F*cked Right

A SPICY NOVELLA

RHIANNA BURWELL

Chapter One

Jace

I fucking hate feeling jealous. I worked hard my entire life to make sure I had everything I wanted because I didn't want to be envious of what someone else had. For something I have worked this hard for, you'd think I'd be better at it, but jealousy has been a bug, buzzing in my ear since the age of sixteen.

When you have a brother in the spotlight, that'll happen. Finn rose to fame when he was barely an adult. With just one video, he went from posting for years with no more than a few views to having a huge following almost overnight. I was a teenager at the time, just getting into my trouble-making years, and although I looked up to Finn, I never felt jealous of him when we were kids.

Until he got famous.

Like every little brother, I always wanted to emulate Finn. I was always taking after him, and I did it well. If he went to basketball camp, I went too, doing just as well as he did, if not better. He never outperformed me, I made sure of it, but his fame was something I couldn't replicate. He worked hard on social media, but I had to accept that a huge part of his success was luck, and that wasn't something I could create out of thin air, no matter how hard I tried. I had never failed at doing what Finn did, but for the first time in my life, I didn't have a choice.

It sounds so stupid when I think about it, the jealousy wrapping around me, but ever since Finn got famous, I felt like I was only his younger brother. I no longer defined myself. I stopped being known as Jace Declan and started being known as Finn Declan's brother. I had none of the success and money that came with fame, but I had all of the shitty consequences.

The biggest one being trust. Trust is a hard thing to come by nowadays because I never know who is using me to get to Finn. It has happened so many times, I now just assume that is why people are nice to me: they know whose brother I am. It's happened with my friends, with potential girlfriends, and even with strangers on the street. I've even had a few professors who gave me extra credit, hoping to get an autograph out of it, just because their kids followed Finn on social media. Every time it happened, it just got more humiliating, and I stopped being able to laugh my way through it.

It was the worst with women. They always *seemed* interested. Always wanted to get to know me more. Always wanted to be brought home to meet my family. But when I saw their eyes light up when Finn would come to visit, I knew it had happened again, and it stung every fucking time.

It fucked me up more than I care to admit. I hated not knowing who to trust, and knowing that Finn was always going to be better than me, always be more desirable, it continued to eat away at me. It just seemed like another area of my life where I wouldn't be able to live up to Finn's successes, so I just stopped. I stopped dating. I stopped trying to find a girlfriend. I stopped the romantic and sexual part of my life altogether, knowing for a fact Finn would always win, no matter what.

It probably didn't help that Finn was the most famous womanizer on our side of the city.

I didn't do it mindfully but watching Finn fuck his way through everyone in town really turned me off from the whole thing. I just stopped wanting to compete when I knew I would lose anyway.

Until Callie that is.

We met in college, in a statistical analysis class. She's been a math whiz since the day she was born, and I noticed her on the first day. Her eyes lit up as she walked into the room, as if it excited her, as if she could actually stomach a two-hour lecture on how to interpret data. I sat next to her the rest of the semester after that, figuring she could help when the class got too hard, and we've been friends since.

I didn't know I wanted her at first. I was so closed off to the whole idea of dating that I became friends with her without even thinking about it. She was funny and kind, and I think I needed a friend more than anything. I didn't think about the fact that her body was my literal wet dream. I didn't think about the fact that when she laughed, she looked right at me, as if she was waiting for me to catch on to the joke, waiting to see if I found it funny too. I didn't think about the fact that she was everything I ever wanted in a woman. I was shut down to the idea completely, and then one day, I woke up and realized that I had an embarrassingly large crush on my best friend, and I was three years too late.

The idea of dating is completely foreign to me now. I was avoiding dating like the plague when I was supposed to be learning how to talk to women, how to flirt. During the time that I should have gained confidence in myself, I was busy trying to pass my college exams. I don't have any practice with women, and now the one I want is the person I have been closest to for the past three years.

Talk about going from zero to sixty.

I've tried to shut the feelings down. Having a thing for my best friend is such a fucking cliché, but I can't stop myself from thinking about the way she looks in a skirt, with her long legs on display. I can't stop myself from fucking my hand to the thought of her bent over the hood of my car, taking my cock, moaning my name. I can't stop thinking about how badly I want her to sit on my face, cumming on top of me.

The stakes are even higher, though, because I like her as a person too. I could see myself dating her. I could see myself lying in bed with her—just enjoying being around her. I could see myself watching stupid TV shows just because they make her happy.

But no one tells you how to navigate these things. There isn't a book called *"How to Figure Out if Your Best Friend Wants to Suck Your Cock 101"* that I can pick up at my local bookstore. Instead of trying to figure my shit out, I wasted time being pissed and jealous of my brother.

Finn fucking Declan. What a dick.

He does one thing right though – he knows how to throw a good fucking party. His engagement party is tonight, and although I'm happy for him, I can't help but feel jealous at the thought of being in his mansion of a house, hiding the fact that I'm still bitter all night. Old habits die hard, but I'm trying like hell to let this one go.

If I have to go and be jealous the whole time, I'm going to get drunk as fuck off his expensive liquor with absolutely no regrets and enjoy my night with Callie, pretending like hell that tonight is an actual date and not just a friendly plus one invite.

At least something good will come out of tonight, even if everything else sucks.

I get to see Callie in a little dress that will probably make my cock hard the entire ride to the party. And–maybe for just a second–I'll pretend that I'm going to be able to take it off of her at the end of the night, because I know that's all I'm going to be able to think about.

Chapter Two

Callie

I blow on the eyelash in front of me, willing the glue to dry faster. I position it on my eye slowly, trying to place it just right. I blink a few times, making sure it is on, and straighten my back before taking in my full appearance. I run my hands down my stomach, willing the nerves to settle, knowing tonight is just like any other, even though it doesn't feel like it.

My brown hair is curled and hangs right below my shoulders. My makeup looks flawless – not that Jace is going to notice. I smooth my hands down my dress, the material clinging to my body like a second skin, the dark green matching well with my dark hair and darker eye makeup. I take in my appearance as a whole, adrenaline running through my body at the prospect of seeing Jace in a situation that feels oddly like a date. I instantly ridicule myself, frustrated that I'm thinking about him when I know I shouldn't be.

It's disgusting to me how long I have been waiting on Jace to make a move. When we first became friends, I thought it was inevitable. I thought he was just waiting for the right time, and eventually, we would find our way to each other. Then, I assumed that he just wanted to get to know me better. It felt like he was just being respectful, treating me like an entire person, and not just something that he wanted to claim. It's been three years now, and I've had to accept that the feelings must be one-sided because if he wanted me, I would know.

It's not like I have been waiting around for him. I've been focusing on myself, dating other people, and trying not to prioritize a relationship in my life. I've been trying to fill my time and forget about the stupid crush, but nothing has worked. No one has been able to take my attention away for more than a few weeks.

I've thought about telling him how I feel a hundred times, but I always back out before I do. We have an amazing friendship, one I'm not sure I want to risk. What if I've made this entire thing up in my head, and he feels nothing for me? I don't want to make things weird between us, but I hate being in this strange in-between.

I walk downstairs, put on a pair of gold strappy heels that make my legs look amazing, and plop on the couch, biding my time until Jace comes to pick me up. I will my nerves to settle, reminding myself that tonight is just like any other.

I can't say I'm not nervous to see Jace dressed up though. That man has been on my mind for almost every single orgasm I've had in the last few years, and the image of him in a dress shirt, with the sleeves rolled up, has made my back arch off my bed several times already.

I try to get myself to stop thinking about it, stop thinking about running my tongue up his chest, tasting his skin, but I can't. His body lives in my head, and every time I try to evict it, it just gets worse, completely consuming me.

The rumble of a car approaches my apartment building, and I rise from the couch, already knowing he's here. Jace usually has a project car he is working on – something he still tries to insist we should do together – and his current one is without a muffler. It's loud enough to hear from a few blocks away.

I grab my water bottle and purse quickly, take a deep breath, and then head out the door, trying to convince myself that tonight is going to be fine. It's not a big deal that it feels like a date. Tonight is going to be like any other, even though we are dressed up and going to an event together...almost like a date. It's fine.

I lock the door behind me, turning toward his car and instantly making eye contact with Jace through the windshield. His eyes glance down my body, just barely, quick enough that I may have imagined it. I breathe out quickly, the warm air around me calming my nerves.

I climb into the truck, my senses being invaded by the smell of Jace. Woodsy and citrus scents wrap around me, completely consuming me. I try to breathe through my mouth, feeling dizzy from being near him, but it still doesn't help. My senses can't seem to process anything other than him. I'm so toast.

"Hey, Cal," Jace quietly greets me as I settle into my seat and close the door. I look over and he's already smiling at me, something that makes my heart rate jump with a nervous flutter.

His eyes connect with mine and I get lost for a second. Deep brown, with flecks of gold, only noticeable if you look closely, if you take your time to appreciate him. He sits with a confidence that everyone can see, his arm resting on his leg making him look particularly sexy. It's just the way he holds himself that shows his confidence. He stares right at me, his eyes fully taking me in, making me feel exposed and seen at the same time. He never shies away from looking at me, something that I'm not sure is a good thing or a bad thing for me.

His brown hair is getting longer, and it is starting to fall into his face. He moves it around quite often, pushing it back when he feels an ounce of uncomfortable feelings. I know he isn't excited about the party tonight because his hair looks mussed, combed through with his fingers several times at this point.

"Hey, you ready?" I ask, trying to dispel some of my nervous energy while buckling into his truck. The seatbelt sits right between my tits, and I see Jace's eyes dip to the cut of my dress, taking in my appearance fully in a way I've never seen from him before. I've never been sure if Jace sees me like that, if he's attracted to me, but his eyes race down my body, examining me with hunger in his eyes. I watch him as he makes his attraction obvious and I feel myself let out a stuttering breath, not knowing what to do with myself.

"Uh, yeah," he mutters as if he lost focus for a second, and I feel my face flush at the thought. He wets his bottom lip with his tongue, and I track the movement, not able to look away. He finally tears his eyes away from me, looking back to my apartment building, his cheeks tinted red.

He is wearing exactly what I expected him to wear, a white dress shirt that looks freshly ironed and a pair of basic black slacks. The sleeves of his shirt are rolled up in a way that makes my mouth literally fucking water.

I try to resist thinking about all of the times I've dragged my hands between my legs, rubbing my clit to the thought of Jace like this. I've thought about this scenario so many times while bringing myself to orgasm, pretending it was Jace's hand working my body. I push the thoughts away, feeling my face heat, but I keep going back to them, unable to stop myself.

Jace goes to turn the truck around, putting his arm on my seat as he turns to look out the back window while he reverses, and I watch intently, his forearm pressing against the sleeve of his shirt, the simple movement driving me crazy. He turns around and starts driving toward Finn's house, and I do my best to pretend I wasn't staring.

The longer we drive, the higher the tension in the car grows. I don't know what's wrong with him, but he grips the steering wheel tightly, his knuckles turning white. He refuses to look at me, just sends me sideways glances now and again. He lightly grinds his jaw together, soft enough that I almost don't notice

I huff out a breath, not understanding what is bugging him so much. He is usually one of the most cool, calm, and collected people I know. "Okay, what's wrong?" I finally ask, turning my entire body toward him, raising my eyebrow in expectation, and willing him to tell me.

"Nothing," he replies, completely avoiding looking at me. I give him my best challenging look, and I know he can see it out of his peripherals, but he avoids it, pretending he can't see it.

"That's how you're gonna be?" I ask, a joking tone to my voice, and he breaks out into a smile instantly, his knuckles loosening on the steering wheel as the tension eases from the car. This is my favorite part of our friendship, when the tension melts away and we can just talk to each other. It's times like these that I remember what is at stake if I confess my feelings. We have this ability to make each other break out of pissed off moods with just a few words, something I have never had with anyone else.

"But, seriously, what's wrong?" I ask again, my tone genuine.

He groans and looks at me again, taking a moment to think before he seems to decide on something. "Okay fine," he says, keeping his eyes on the road. "It's just always a little annoying to be around Finn. He always got everything he ever wanted and it's tough to compete," he admits, his voice shy, reserved, as if this is something he doesn't want to say out loud.

I do my best to be a good friend, resisting the urge to reach out and comfort him with my touch, but come up blank, not knowing how to make this situation better. "He doesn't have *everything*," I urge, trying my best to be helpful. He looks over at me, his eyes piercing my entire soul, with a look that says, *"seriously?"*, and I laugh instantly. "Okay, yeah, that was bad. I just mean that he doesn't have everything *you* want, ya know?" I say, shifting my gaze out the window, not able to look at him anymore without appreciating every inch. This conversation is too intense and it just makes me want to comfort him all of the ways I'm best at, naked and with my tongue.

"What doesn't he have?" he asks, his voice sounding smooth and rich, yet hoarse almost, and it makes me rub my thighs together, just enough to soothe the ache that I've had since I got into Jace's truck. I look over at him and catch him looking over at my legs. He looks away quickly, and I stare at him for a second, trying to read his expression, trying to understand what he is thinking but I can't.

"Privacy, freedom," I answer, knowing I have a good point, knowing I'm right. "His life comes at a cost, and you know that better than anyone." Jace has seen firsthand what happens when someone becomes famous. Finn went from being a normal person with an everyday life to someone that was known by the world. He went from being able to walk down the street, to being recognized instantly, anywhere he went. Jace told me before that it was fun for him at first, but after a while, you just want that privacy back again.

"Yeah, I know," Jace says as he moves, his head from side to side as if he is letting the thought move around in there. "It's just annoying that I have to deal with some of the downfalls of being famous without any of the money or respect, ya know?"

"I know. It sucks. But, you know that you could ask Finn for anything. He knows what a pain in the ass his fame has been for you. He'd buy you a sports car if you asked for it," I say, remembering on several occasions when Finn would offer to buy Jace high ticket items. Finn has never been stingy with his money, especially when his family is concerned. His fame doesn't just affect him, and he does what he can to acknowledge that. Finn is honestly a good guy, he just got thrown into a weird situation.

"The things I want can't be bought," he answers, his voice barely audible. I glance over at him, confused, not understanding what he is talking about anymore.

"What do you mean?" I ask. "What do you want that can't be bought?" He looks at me, his eyes darting between me and the road, with a small amount of panic inside of them. I stare back, trying to read his gaze for any hint of what is going on. He opens his mouth to speak but closes it, no words escaping. Stopping at a stop sign, his eyes search mine, looking for something, and then dip to my mouth. He rubs his lips together and my eyes track the movement, completely transfixed by him.

"Nothing, never mind," he breathes, looking back at the road, his eyes not returning to mine. I can tell by his voice that he isn't going to bring it up again, that I should just let it go, but I don't want to. I want to know what he was going to say.

I turn and look out the window, doing my best to let it go, knowing I won't get answers even if I keep asking. Yet that doesn't stop my brain from working overtime, half hoping and half forcing myself not to hope.

Chapter Three

Jace

Callie's dress is going to fucking melt my goddamn brain. I haven't been able to think straight since she got into the truck, and it only gets worse the longer she sits next to me. I've been on edge, doing my best to conceal my hard cock, not wanting her to see how much she turns me on.

For the last few months, I think I've done a good job covering up my attraction but this dress is ruining all of my resolve. I don't know how the fuck I am supposed to keep my hands to myself when she looks like she was sculpted by the gods. I have half a mind to skip the party altogether and just beg her to let me worship her body the way it deserves, giving it my attention well into the night.

I look over at her, not even knowing what to say. I wish I was better with my words. I wish I didn't freeze up when she was around me. I never seem to be able to think when she is around, and now I can't even look at her without needing to hold back a groan.

The dress leaves very little to the imagination, hugging her body like it was made for her. Her full hips fill out the dress in a way that makes my hands ache with the need to grab her, to feel her skin on my own. The forest green color contrasts with her dark hair and dark eyes, making her look like a fucking dream.

I wouldn't have invited her if I knew she was going to look this good. Honestly, I'm regretting that decision a little bit right now as I white-knuckle the steering wheel, unable to even glance in her direction.

I stare at the road ahead of me, desperate to calm myself down. My cock is already hard, and I know I need to stop thinking about how amazing she looks or it won't go away all night. If I don't stop now, tonight is going to be agony, thinking of all the ways I want to please her, and finally show her with my body how I feel.

I keep my eyes ahead, knowing if I look at her, I'm going to blurt out every thought in my head. If I look at her long legs again, I'm going to confess how many times I've thought about her wrapped around me while I fucked my own hand, moaning her name in the shower, thinking of only her.

I finally pull into Finn's driveway, successfully avoiding looking at Callie for the rest of the drive. The driveway is long, almost a mile, which was Finn's main reason for buying the house in the first place. Privacy was a huge factor; I've heard him talk about putting a gate out front a few times.

He never used to care about privacy until he met Emma. I mean he hated when people stood around his house, waiting to catch a glance at the man himself, but he never felt unsafe. The second he started seeing Emma he shifted his perspective, becoming extremely protective. It would almost be sweet if it didn't make me want to throw up.

I pull up to the house, put the car into park, and keep my eyes forward. "Ready to go?" Callie asks, and I find myself drawn to look at her before I even have the chance to stop myself. A small smile graces her lips and I take her in, fully, appreciating every piece of her, wanting to commit the details to my memory, as if they weren't already there.

I want her more than I've wanted anything in my entire life, but Callie is also my best friend. She's always in my corner, always on my side. She doesn't always agree with me, but she will stick up for me around anyone, making sure they know where she stands. She is beautiful and smart and everything I have ever wanted in a person.

But I can't have her.

At least that is what I keep telling myself.

"Let's go," I cough out, opening my door and looking away. It feels like a rock has sunk into my stomach. I push it away, not wanting to deal with it right now. We both step out of my truck, Callie hopping out more than anything, and we make our way to the giant house in front of us.

Sitting at seven bedrooms and eight baths – why he needs more bathrooms than bedrooms is beyond me – the house is as tall as it is wide. It had a modern look to it: all white and clean-looking siding lines the outside, making it feel warm while also regal at the same time. The windows are big, giving a lot of natural light to the inside. The grass around the house is always cut to perfection, and the entire estate looks clean and proper, something that Finn has never been. The pool that wraps around the house is a little much for my taste, especially because I know Finn doesn't like to swim, but nothing is too good for my brother.

"I can't wait to see the ring. I bet it's a fucking rock," Callie says, meeting me at the front bumper so we can walk in together. I tuck away the jealousy swarming through me, knowing I need to leave it at the door and be happy for my brother and his future wife.

We make our way to the door, ringing the doorbell as we take in the beauty of the house. I've been here before but never paid it much mind. This time though, I have things to avoid looking at, so I look at the house suddenly extremely interested in every single detail.

I look over at Callie, just for a second, not able to help myself. She stares at the house, bewilderment in her eyes while the sun shines over her, and I get lost in the sight, unable to take my eyes off of her. I open my mouth to speak, not even knowing what I'm going to say, but the door bursts open instead, interrupting whatever I was about to say.

"Oh my god, you guys look so cute!" Emma exclaims, the door opening fast and smooth. I warn Emma to stop with my eyes, willing her not to make things more awkward than they already are for Callie and me. She's wanted us to get together since the first time she met Callie and even though we have insisted that we are just friends, it's like she can see right through us.

Emma has acted like my sister since she started dating Finn. I was used to a certain kind of woman that hung around him, snotty and entitled, but Emma surprised me. She was nice from the first second we met, greeting me as if she had known me for years, making me feel comfortable around her. She has this way about her that is zero bullshit. She is fiery and warm, her red hair matching her personality almost perfectly.

"You guys look amazing!" Emma says, her eyes darting between both of us with a hint of mischief in her gaze, but I ignore it, already knowing what she is thinking.

"Let me see the ring," Callie blurts out as if she couldn't wait to ask. Emma became like a sister to me, but she became a friend to Callie too. Emma holds out her hand to show the small diamond sitting on her ring finger, small enough that it surprises me. I'm not one to be materialistic, but I know what Finn could afford, and it is a lot more than that.

"That's how everyone looks at it," Emma says with a smile, her voice radiating humor and understanding all in one. "I didn't want anything too big. I wouldn't have felt right getting a big diamond. I barely feel good about living in this beautiful house. I didn't want him to spend someone's income on a ring." I feel myself smile, my respect for her only increasing. It's still shocking to me that she is with my brother. Finn always felt bad about a lot of things that his fame brought on our family, but his money has never been one of them. He has no problem spending money and spending a lot of it. I can already imagine Emma challenging him on that, and the thought of my brother being put in his place makes me laugh a little to myself.

"Well, come join the party!" Emma says while leading the way into their house. I've been here a few times before but not enough to know my way around. From the outside, it looks decently sized, but from the inside, it looks like a fucking mansion, a place you could get lost in.

The house opens up into an entryway that is about the size of my apartment. Hooks for jackets hang to my right, and cubbies for countless shoes sit to my left, making the space feel homey instead of cluttered. The light in the room is what draws you in. The walls are all white, the natural light bouncing off of them and making the space look brighter. The space is lived in but not cluttered, clean but not spotless. There are things dotting the counters all around us, but they look like they have a purpose and order.

In front of the entryway is a hallway that leads to the kitchen, lined with pictures of Finn and Emma on various vacations, my brother smiling more than I have ever seen. Emma leads us into the kitchen while Callie stares around her. While she looks at everything, I look at her, desperate to look where she is looking, wanting to see the home the same way that she does. I glance at her and then follow her gaze trying to find the thing that amazes her and puts that beautiful, stunned look on her face. Her brown hair frames her face perfectly as she takes the entire house in, her eyes wide, and all I can imagine is grabbing her hair in my fist and crashing our mouths together. She walks around the space effortlessly as if she belongs here, and I want, with every fiber of my being, to give her something like this.

I try not to think about the fact that I won't ever be able to give her a home like this. I push the feeling away, wanting, just for tonight, to feel as if I could deserve her someday.

We make our way into the entertainment room – at least that is what Emma calls it. You could fit a whole house in this room alone. It is bright and white, like most of the house, making it feel welcoming and open but also clean and modern. There are a few couches in the middle, making the shape of a box. The room is almost full of people, people I have never met before. Bartenders that Finn must have hired sit behind the bar in the back of the room, all making drinks, rushing around, and trying to manage the crowd surrounding the bar, desperate for a drink. The room vibrates with energy, the sound of voices becoming more of a hum than anything.

"Nice, huh? I told Finn getting new couches and adding the bar would be a nice touch for the party," Emma says, looking at the room with pride, as if she has slowly made it hers. "You wanna do shots?" Emma whispers to Callie, leaning over to her like they have been friends for ages. Callie looks at me, looking for confirmation that she can step away with Emma. I just nod, seeing my brother across the room and knowing I should go say hi.

Callie walks away, her ass and hips swaying, and I can't help but imagine sinking my fingers into her hips, leaving marks that she could find the next morning. I can't fucking look away. I stare, my cock growing hard in my slacks, knowing I'm going to be thinking about her in that goddamn dress all night if I don't stop now. But I keep staring, unable and unwilling to take my eyes off of her.

She turns around suddenly and I straighten, my face heating with embarrassment, knowing she caught me staring at her ass. She sends a small smile, her eyes connecting with mine before getting lost in the crowd.

I try to stop thinking about it. I try to, if not erase then at least, tame my thoughts of her, but it doesn't work. I think about that goddamn smile. My eyes linger on the location where she just stood, willing her to reappear just so I can see her again.

I'm going to need a fucking drink if I'm going to get through tonight.

I turn toward where I saw Finn, intent on finding as many drinks as humanly possible. I know I can't have her no matter how badly I want her, and I can't deal with that while sober.

Chapter Four

Callie

J ace takes another shot, and I watch him from the other side of the room, never letting him fully out of my sight. I talk to someone that knows Finn and Emma – I think Emma's cousin or something – but I can't focus on what the woman in front of me is saying. Jace keeps looking over at me with eyes that are glassy and full of need, and it is throwing me completely off balance.

Jace has never looked at me like that. He never showed any interest in me physically. Sure, he has checked me out a few times, a lingering gaze here or there, but nothing more than that. He put me in the friendship category from the beginning, at least that's how it felt, but tonight, something has changed.

He keeps looking over at me with hungry eyes drinking me in and not being shy about it.

I glance back over at him as his eyes scan down my body, never resting on one area, seeming to consume my entire frame, lust radiating off of him. His tongue pops out, wetting his bottom lip, and, even from across the room, I feel the movement with my entire body.

I wait for him to come over to me, to tell me what is going on in his head, but his feet stay planted on the ground, never moving closer, never finding their way to me. I keep talking to the woman in front of me and Emma, laughing and smiling when appropriate, but my mind is on Jace.

The party reduces to a simmer. Only a few people still mingle around. As people leave, they drop envelopes on the table designated for gifts. I find the practice of giving Finn and Emma cash almost funny. If you spend a second looking around the house, you would see that they don't need any more money, but it isn't really about that when it comes to rich people, is it?

I feel Jace in my peripheral vision while watching people leave. I watch him appreciatively while he isn't looking, admiring the man who I've known for years. I watch his head tilt back with laughter when someone makes a joke, a joke I'm not close enough to hear, and I smile, his laughter contagious. He has this easy-going way about him that warms the room with his presence, while also making me want to rip his clothes off and see what it takes to wipe the smile from his face.

I watch as Jace thanks the bartender from across the room, lifting his shot to his lips and tipping his head back, swallowing in one gulp. I watch him talk to the man next to him, confidence surrounding him that makes a shiver run through me. I will myself to focus on what Emma is saying next to me, but I can't. I feel completely captivated by him. I can feel the tension between us, the muscles in my core aching.

Jace turns toward me, his eyes connecting with mine instantly, as if he knew where to find me. He looks at me with determination as his eyes trail up and down my body. He mutters something, something that looks a whole lot like "fuck it", but he's too far away for me to hear.

He starts walking over to me, looking at me like I am a prime steak and he is fucking starving, a look that makes me forget to breathe, more from anticipation than fear. My body mirrors his as he approaches, ready for what he is going to say, ready for what is finally going to happen between us, because deep in my soul, I think a part of me knew this was always going to happen. We would find our way to each other eventually, even when it felt hopeless.

Finn comes out of nowhere and suddenly stops him. He says something to Jace, putting his hand on his shoulder, steadying him slightly, the alcohol seemingly catching up to him. Finn glances over at me and shakes his head at Jace as he says something to him, his entire body language protective, with just a hint of condescension, something that I know will drive Jace insane. Jace replies to him, his face contouring into anger and annoyance and Finn replies, his body language going stiff. I watch with curiosity and concern, the exchange getting more heated the longer it goes on. Jace angrily pushes Finn's arm off of him. Finn throws his hands in the air, and their voices get louder.

My eyes dart to Emma, and hers connect with mine. We speak silently for just a second, communicating with nothing but subtle eye movements, and then start walking over together, knowing we need to calm them down before this escalates into something more serious.

We walk up quickly, the pit in my stomach growing, not knowing what we are going to walk into. The exchange between brothers only continues to intensify, Jace yells something at Finn with slurred speech, his voice deep and rough.

"C'mon, man. That's not what I meant, and you know it," Finn says sternly as he rolls his eyes. Jace instantly gets in his face, challenging him but Finn doesn't back down, not in his own house, not at his own party.

"What the fuck did you mean then? You just don't want me to have anything, do you?" Jace spits out, only inches away from Finn at this point, and I know they are both seconds away from throwing a punch.

I step in between them, not even thinking about it honestly. I just know this needs to stop. They are both drunk and pissed, and this won't help a damn thing.

"Walk away," I say sternly, looking Finn directly in the eyes while he stares at Jace, venom in his gaze. I challenge him, and after a few seconds, his gaze drops to me, as if he is finally seeing me. He looks over to Emma, who has her hands on his chest, trying to pull him away from the chaos. I shoot Emma an apologetic look, and she nods, pulling Finn away from the middle of the room. Finn deflates into her touch, as if her touch grounds him, bringing him back down to earth. "C'mon," I say, putting my hands on Jace's chest, trying to comfort him too. I lead him away from the party, finding a hallway leading to god knows where but knowing he needs a second to cool off. I walk us down the hallway for a few minutes, wanting to get away from the noise of the party completely.

"He is fucking lucky you stepped in, or I would've had him on the ground," he says through gritted teeth, the alcohol running through his veins seeming to disappear, the fight sobering him. I put my hands on his chest again, wanting to comfort him with my touch although annoyance rolls through me. I don't know what was said, but initiating a fistfight with Finn isn't normal behavior for Jace, even when he's drunk.

"What the fuck is wrong with you?" I hiss. He works hard to keep his head down, never picking fights like that, with anyone, much less his brother. The behavior is so unlike him, and I don't understand what could make him so pissed off that he was ready to throw a punch.

"Nothing," he mumbles, shutting down, shutting me out. He stares at the ground, avoiding eye contact, but I can feel what he's feeling. I feel the rage and disappointment running off of him. I feel his sadness and jealousy, and for once, just once, I want him to tell me how he is feeling. I want him to let it all out and finally let me into what is going on inside of his head.

"Are you *that* jealous of him? You want to beat his ass for having more than you?" I say angrily, knowing I'm pushing him. I don't know how else to get him to open up. I know if I push him hard enough, he will break and his emotions will spill out of him. I know I probably shouldn't, but I do it anyway. "Ya know what, go ahead. I won't stop you this time. I won't save you before Finn puts *your* ass on the floor," I say, unleashing every emotion in my body, letting it spill out of me without an ounce of remorse. I watch him as his eyes darken, the dam inside of him seeming to break.

"He has everything, Callie. Fucking everything!" Jace yells, his voice full of hurt and betrayal, and anger all in one. He runs his hands through his hair, frustrated and working through his emotions, seeming to lose the battle against himself. "He has everything, and then he tells me I can't go after you? That I can't finally tell you how I feel? Why? Because I'm drunk? He's gonna sit there and tell me I can't go after the one fucking thing I actually want?" he yells, his face red, anger and pain etched into his face. He slumps against the wall, all of the energy suddenly leeching out of him. I play the words back in my head, trying to get them to make sense, but I just can't seem to.

I stare at him as he huffs out breaths, seeming to come down from the emotional high. He stares at the floor, avoiding eye contact, shaking his head as if he is going through the entire conversation again inside of his head. I watch him, willing his body to explain to me what the fuck is going on.

Our friendship has always been reliable, always been consistent. I always knew Jace's next steps, but tonight is nothing but a shock. The air around us has changed, and I'm not sure what to expect.

It feels like the words click in my mind all at once, my body stiffening. He said exactly what I think he did, and I don't know what it means. I stare at him, and his eyes slowly meet mine, meaning and understanding written all over them as he waits for my reaction.

I knew this would happen eventually, a part of me always knew, but I didn't know it would happen now. I didn't realize when I got into his truck tonight that we were going to hit a crossroads and everything would be laid out.

"You want me?" I ask, my voice barely even a whisper. He stares into my eyes, his chest still heaving with deep breaths. I track the movements in his eyes as they search my face. He looks so uncertain all of a sudden, all of the anger gone leaving only vulnerability. The adrenaline of the situation is used up, and I don't know what we are going to do without it.

I stare and I wait, willing him to answer faster, needing an answer right now. My mind is spinning, giving me all of the reasons this might not even be real, why I might be making this entire thing up. Maybe he just likes the way I look tonight, the dress finally accenting the attraction we have toward each other. Maybe he is just drunk, not even knowing what he is saying. Maybe his emotions are just heightened because Finn is getting married and he isn't sure how to handle that. Maybe I am just dreaming, and I'm going to wake up, wet and horny, wishing this night was real.

"You want me?" I ask again, pleading, needing an answer to stop the spiral from happening inside of my head. My voice comes out louder this time, the sound bouncing off the walls and consuming me. I stare into his brown eyes, and his mouth opens to speak. I feel my heartbeat pick up, not even able to guess what he is about to say.

"You guys want to play some drinking games?" Emma asks, turning the corner into the hallway that I dragged us into. Jace and I turn away from each other instantly, my entire body shifting, feeling as if we got caught in a compromising position. Emma's eyes bounce in between both of us. "Sorry, was I interrupting?" she asks, a wince forming on her face as she takes in the situation. Her red hair is illuminated by the lights coming from the party, and I stare at it, needing somewhere to look other than at Jace.

"No, not at all," Jace replies, his words sounding strong, a small punch to the gut. I glance over at him, hoping he will communicate with his eyes, and finally answer the question I asked, but he doesn't even look at me. He stares at Emma and ignores my gaze, and I feel my stomach sink. "Yeah, let's do it," he replies to her question, moving instantly, a newfound energy in his step as he follows her back to the party, leaving me in the hallway alone, feeling stupid and hurt while the darkness consumes me.

I feel like I made this entire thing up in my head, and the self-doubt is eating me alive. He never even answered my question, but somehow, in a roundabout way, it feels like he did. No answer is an answer – it just wasn't the answer I wanted.

I give myself a few seconds to be sad, knowing I need to return to the party, and then I lift my chin, move my shoulders back, and follow them back into the entertainment room. I leave my hope back in that hallway, finally giving myself permission to let this stupid crush go because it seems that he already has.

Chapter Five

Jace

I'm such a dickhead. I know I should've answered her, but I didn't know how. I didn't even mean to say what I said, it just came out, and then I didn't know what to do. The second the words were out of my mouth, I wanted to rip them back from her ears, going back in time. She looked at me, and I couldn't read her. I didn't want to tell her how I feel, I already felt too exposed, so I just shut down, and now I feel like an ass. I *am* an ass.

I walk back into the room, everyone's eyes darting at me as I enter. I try to walk confidently through the room, not letting people's gaze influence me, but shame still wraps its way around me, reminding me that I made a fool out of myself just moments ago. I walk up to Finn, knowing I should apologize.

"Hey, dude, we good?" I ask, already seeming to know that we are. This is how we have always gotten over fights. We don't need to talk it out. We don't need to explain what the fuck happened. It was just drunk bullshit anyway, nothing worth holding a grudge over.

"Yeah, man, we're good," he says, a cheeky smile on his face, a contrast from the look of rage he had just fifteen minutes ago. We do a man-back-slap-hug and part, and I know we are back to normal, the stupid ass fight completely forgotten about.

I feel Callie behind me before I see her, her presence making my entire body tense, but I push it away, knowing that I didn't deserve her before, but now I *really* don't. I couldn't even answer a simple question. I couldn't just say "fuck it" for a second and tell her how badly I want her. I couldn't express everything I've been feeling, the ways my eyes never seem to leave her body, the way her laugh warms my fucking soul, the way I am calmed by just her presence. She deserves someone who will shout it from the rooftops, and I'm not that guy.

If I were honest with myself, I would realize that I don't deserve her either way, whether I become that guy or not. I know that now more than ever. Sitting in the house that my brother earned, looking at the fame and fortune he acquired, I know Callie deserves someone who will give her this life, and

I can't. She deserves someone who can spoil her and make her comfortable, and that person will never be me.

I don't even know how to fuck her right. I don't know how to make her cum on my face, moaning my name while her back arches as I suck on her clit. I don't know how to fuck her until she's cumming, tightening around me until she milks the cum out of my cock.

I don't deserve to date her, and I *definitely* don't deserve to fuck her.

I have nothing to offer her, so I don't know why I thought for a second she would ever want *me*. It doesn't matter that I didn't answer her, because at the end of the day, she deserves every little thing the world has, and I don't know the first thing about giving her that.

"You wanna play never have I ever or something?" Emma asks, looking around the room at the people still mingling around, most of which are the closest people to Finn and Emma. As I look around, I make eye contact with Callie. My gaze runs down her body, almost like it is a force of habit. I look away quickly, knowing I have no right to admire her. I feel her eyes on me, but I ignore them, not wanting to see how my actions have influenced her.

I look back at Emma and nod, answering her question with a tense smile. I don't necessarily want to play, but I want space from the conversation I just didn't have with Callie. I need something to fill the air around me, something to take Callie off of my mind, and if that means I play a stupid fucking party game, I couldn't care less anymore. Part of me just wants to say fuck it and leave, but I can't stomach the idea of sitting in the car with her, completely alone, her presence eating me alive.

I grab a drink, which of course is an extremely expensive liquor because Finn is too good for anything other than the top shelf, and make my way into the circle that Emma has created. Everyone is sitting on the floor and getting cozy with each other, but I feel like I'm not inside my body. I feel like I'm still in that hallway staring at Callie, not knowing what to say.

I sit next to Callie, not wanting to abandon her since she doesn't know anyone else here. I hate to admit that her presence also just comforts me. I enjoy being around her, but I can't think of that right now without thinking about all the things I wish I would have said in that hallway, so I tuck the emotions away and focus on everyone around me instead.

"Okay, everyone has played this right? You know the rules?" Emma asks, looking around the small circle of about ten people. I don't know the other people well. I've seen a few of them at other parties Finn and Emma have had, but I'm not even on a first-name basis with them. Finn and Emma sit together, right next to me, and Callie sits on my left. I don't pay much attention to anyone else, my body seeming to be tuned into Callie, something I wish I could turn off right now.

"You drink when you've done it, right?" Callie asks next to me, her voice sounding small and sad. It feels like a punch to the gut, knowing that I was the reason for it. I hate that I did that to her. I hate that I made her feel that way. I hate that I couldn't just tell her the truth. I take a drink from my cup, needing something to wash away the shame.

"Exactly. We go around the circle saying things we haven't done with the intention of trying to get people to drink," Emma explains, and then gestures to Callie, seemingly indicating for her to start the game

"Uhm, okay," Callie says hesitantly, looking around the room, nervousness dancing in her eyes until they settle on Emma and a mischievous smile crosses her lips. "Never have I ever been proposed to," she says, raising her eyebrows at Emma and waiting for her to drink.

Emma rolls her eyes with a smile, bringing the cup to her mouth and drinking. She looks lovingly at Finn, and he smiles at her. I look away, telling myself it is because I don't want to interrupt their moment, but really the jealousy that is wracking through my body is consuming me. I want what they have.

"Okay, my turn," the blonde girl next to Callie mutters, looking around nervously. I think her name is Clover or something, but I can't remember. I stare at her, willing my attention not to drift to Callie, but it does, naturally.

Her legs are crossed in front of her, and my eyes trail them up and down, taking in her body as a whole and salivating over her like a fucking dog. When she sits, her stomach poaches a little, and all I want to do is admire her, run my fingers over the smooth skin, enjoying every single ounce of her, because I know I would. I crave her body like it was made for me. I imagine running my tongue over her skin, taking my time with her, and the thought makes my cock grow hard.

"Never have I ever done anal," Clover says finally, her face going red as she looks around the room, waiting for people's reactions. A few people drink, but I keep my eyes away from Finn and Emma, not even wanting to know, but that keeps my line of vision on Callie. She brings the cup up to her lips, taking a sip and I stare, completely transfixed by her mouth. My cock throbs in my pants, unable to get the image of her bent over, looking back at me with her head on the bed, and my finger stretching her ass open. God, she would look so good laid out like that. I would line my cock up to her ass, ready to feel how fucking tight that hole can get while she begs for it, begs for me to make her feel good.

Jesus Christ. I need a cold shower.

"Let's make this easy. I want to get drunk," the body-builder-looking guy next to Clover mutters, looking around the room with a glint in his eye, as if he knows something we don't. "Never have I ever had sex," he says confidently, instantly taking the cup in front of him and drinking himself, almost as if to reassure the room that he has in fact done it.

My body goes rigid instantly, and I feel my face flaming red. A few people around the room laugh, everyone raising their cups to their lips, giving the bodybuilder a hard time since he picked something so easy.

The cup stays in my hand, not moving. I'm not sure what to do. Callie raises her cup, takes a drink, and then looks over at me. I feel her gaze on me instantly, but my body won't move. I tell myself to just drink, just pretend, but the cup stays where it is, in my hand for the entire room to see.

Everyone has drank at this point, and they mingle back and forth, seemingly oblivious to the war raging within me. I wait for someone to say something, for someone to notice the panic on my face and the cup still sitting in my hand, but no one looks at me.

No one but Callie.

I watch from the corner of my eye as Callie's face scrunches into confusion, and then realization, her mouth opening as if a thought has just suddenly hit her.

I raise the cup, my arm finally working with me, pulling a swig into my mouth, knowing I would rather be a liar than be made fun of for this. I swallow, the liquor barely making its way down my throat as it tightens with worry. I ignore Callie's gaze, the shock on her face, willing her to forget she saw anything. I start to prepare lies, needing a plan when she comes to me and asks what happened, but my mind is completely blank, somehow knowing I won't be able to get out of this without telling her the truth.

I may have just hidden my secret from the rest of the group, but Callie knows. She knows that I'm a virgin, and I honestly thought the humiliation tonight couldn't get any worse. Guess I was wrong.

Chapter Six

Callie

The party continues on as if nothing happened, but I know what I saw, and I'm still working on picking up my jaw off the floor. The more I think about it, the more it makes sense. I have never seen Jace with a woman. He never talks about dating or his sex life, and I always just assumed it was because he was more reserved. I liked that he didn't talk about other women, because honestly, I didn't wanna hear about someone with him when I couldn't stop fantasizing about riding his cock while holding his hands down, not allowing him to touch me.

But now it feels like all the pieces have clicked together, and a lot of things make more sense now.

I knew about his jealousy of Finn for a while now. We don't talk about his family often, but when we do, there is always a small part of him that gets a little bitter. It's subtle. You would only notice if you were looking, but I've always suspected there was something deeper there, and it feels like it makes more sense now. Finn has always played the field, being known for fucking multiple women every month. He's been on the front page of almost every news site with his hand around a new shoulder, and that's a hard act to follow. I can't imagine being Finn's brother in a society that glorifies men for having as much sex as possible.

The game continues around the room, and I try to listen, try to tune back into what people are saying, but I can't listen more than to figure out when I need to drink. I'm stuck on this idea, and although realization and understanding are surging through my body, lust consumes me. I rub my thighs together, desperate for any kind of friction. I can feel my nipples pebbling in my shirt, and I do my best to ignore it, to do my best to focus on what is happening, but I can't.

The idea of being the first woman to slide my pussy along his cock, finally allowing him to feel what it is like to be inside, makes heat rush between my legs, demanding my attention.

The idea of him begging, pleading for it even, fuck. I can't even think with that floating around my head.

I have always wanted to fuck Jace. There was always something about him that makes my skin prick, but the idea of him being desperate to finally feel what it is like to be inside of a cunt makes my entire body light up.

I can feel my face flushing, and I don't care. I can't get the idea of being the first person to fuck Jace Declan out of my mind. Putting my tongue on his cock, running it up the length, letting him feel the back of my throat, maybe even letting him cum in my mouth but making him beg for it first.

Shit, I need to stop thinking about this.

We are friends. We have always been friends. I don't want to cross this line with him, especially after the stunt in the hallway. It is too likely to ruin the friendship we have. I don't want to lose him, and it isn't worth it just to hear him whisper my name, pleading with me to finally make him feel good...right?

Even as I try to talk myself out of it, I can't even convince myself. It feels like a lie that I'm telling myself. I have never wanted someone as much as I want him right now. I have never been this wound up, desperate for someone to just fucking touch me, and part of me thinks that it would be worth it. It would be worth it to say fuck it and risk it all but a small drop of doubt stops me. I feel like I'm teetering right between both decisions, not knowing which way to lean.

The party wraps up slowly, too slow for my liking. My head feels jumbled, and I just want to clear the air with Jace. I want to get everything out, once and for all, but Jace seems to have different plans. After the incident in the hallway, I didn't want to get drunk. I knew I would say something I didn't want to say, but Jace seems to have other plans. He looks at me with pain and lust and need in his eyes, and then takes a shot as if his thoughts are too much to handle. He stares at my body like it owns him like it's consuming his every thought. I stare back, willing him to understand that I feel it too, that I feel this desperate and primal urge to be around him, to be consumed by him, but he never looks at me long enough to see it. He isn't completely drunk, teetering right on the edge, but he is drunk enough that I know we won't have an honest conversation tonight.

"Hey, you guys just want to crash in the guest rooms? It's late, and you probably shouldn't drive," Emma mutters next to me, her voice thick with exhaustion and alcohol. Her eyes dart between Jace and me, waiting for an answer. I look at Jace, not really caring what we do. He takes a second to answer, probably trying to process his thoughts with six shots of Grey Goose running through his bloodstream.

"Uh," Jace mutters, looking at me, looking for an answer. I shrug. At this point, I just want to go to bed and forget tonight ever happened. "Yeah, that's fine," he says, his voice tired. People mill out of the house slowly, receiving half-hearted goodbyes when they do, until it is just Jace and me, and Emma and Finn in the house.

We help Finn and Emma clean the place up. It's easier to just get it done now. Even though Finn is as rich as he is, he isn't above a red solo cup, and right now they litter his kitchen table and living room floor. Everyone's exhaustion seeps into the room, making just as much of a mess as the party did.

It doesn't take long until the entertainment room looks normal again, and I stifle a yawn while I look at Jace for confirmation that we can go to bed. He nods at me, and we start making our way to the guest rooms. Emma gives us directions to the guest rooms, running and grabbing me a set of her pajamas to sleep in.

The hallway off the kitchen leads to the bedrooms, but it is long, so Jace and I walk side by side, silently. The silence feels like it is eating me up, the walls caving in on us, pushing us closer together and making it harder to breathe.

I'm so aware of his presence, especially with his body right next to mine, his arm pressed against my skin. I can feel the heat coming off of him, making my entire body feel warm, feel needy.

I imagine, just for a second, what would happen if I slipped into his bedroom. I imagine how he would run his hands down my body, desperate for me to finally show him what it is like to a fuck a woman. I would take control the first time, showing him what I want and what I need, but the second time, I would let him take me any way he wants. I would let him appreciate my body how he wants to, the way his eyes have been begging me to finally let him.

I try to push the thoughts away as we reach two doors next to each other −our rooms for the night − but the thoughts stubbornly stay at the front of my mind. I don't know where he is at, but I know where I'm at. I want him. I've been waiting for him to make a move for a while, desperate for him to confess how he feels, but maybe I should stop waiting. Maybe he needs me to take control instead.

"Night," Jace mutters, barely looking me in the eye, and opening his door. He turns to leave, and the urge to say something takes over my body. My entire world has been flipped on its head today. My emotions are running wild. I want to escape to my room, I want to sleep it off, but more than that, I want to talk to my best friend.

"Hey," I say suddenly, grabbing his arm lightly, knowing I will regret it if I don't say something. Sparks shoot down my hand instantly and my entire body pulses. I watch Jace flinch, his face looking pained by my touch. "Are we okay?" I ask, my voice sounding small, too small for my liking, but I don't care.

He turns to me, his face morphing into every emotion, but I can't read them fully. His eyes glaze over my body, seeming to take in every inch, soaking me in completely. I feel my heart rate increase, not knowing what to make of his hesitation.

He sighs, seeming to come to terms with something. "No, we aren't okay," he mutters, and my stomach drops, completely falling through the floor. I look at him with confusion, not knowing what he even means. I never wanted to lose my best friend during this, and the thought that I might have makes my heart hurt.

"Why not?" I ask, not knowing how to say all of the things I want to, the moment feeling too big, but knowing I need answers.

"I know what you saw, Callie," he mutters, his voice coming out with a hint of disgust, his lip curling as he speaks, as if he is ashamed of himself. "I'm not good enough for you," he whispers quietly enough that I barely hear him. The words hang in the air, soaking up all of the oxygen in the hallway, consuming me.

"That's not true," I say, shaking my head, not knowing what to say, not knowing how to fix this, but knowing that he is wrong. I just don't know how to get him to believe that.

"It is," he confirms, looking at me with determination in his eyes. "We can't be together, Callie, no matter how often you look at me with those fucking eyes. No matter how often I imagine what you would feel like underneath me, claiming me like you own me," he says, and I feel goosebumps trail down my arms, desperate to play out his wildest fantasies but knowing now isn't the time to be thinking like this.

I open my mouth to speak, to fight against what he is saying, but he holds his hand up, shutting me down. I close my mouth and wait for him to speak again, already knowing I'm not going to like what he has to say. "I don't think I could just have you for the night, Callie. You are completely consuming," he says while letting out a breath as if he is finally telling the truth. "It won't work, and you know it. I can't lose you as a friend, so please, please, just let this go," he pleads, looking at me with such desperation in his gaze that I have no words. I feel the fight inside of me fizzle, wanting to protect him and this friendship more than make my point.

I nod, feeling defeated. "Okay," I mutter, my gaze landing on the floor, not wanting to look at him right now.

He leans forward, the heat of his body washing over me. My breath hitches, my entire being responding to him, wanting him. But instead of satisfying me, he plants a kiss on my forehead before moving away from me and entering his room for the night.

I hear his door click shut, his presence gone from the hallway, before taking a staggered breath, not knowing what to make out of this night, not knowing how to prove that he is wrong about us, that he is wrong about himself.

Chapter Seven

Jace

I can't sleep after what happened in the hallway. Hours pass as my mind races, running through if turning her down was a good idea, stopping what she was going to say, and the longer I lay here, with a hard cock, the longer it feels like a mistake.

The truth is, my friendship with Callie has never been entirely platonic. It's always felt a little more than that, but I couldn't admit it. I couldn't admit that I've always had feelings for her, I just wasn't aware of it. I pushed them down for years, pretending that friendship feels like this.

But now that I know, I want to pretend I didn't, because this means we could actually be something, and that terrifies me more than anything. I'm not ready to face all the things that make me feel insecure, and being with someone as amazing as Callie, would bring that all up to the surface. I want to be the kind of person that is okay with that, but if I'm real with myself, I don't know if I would be able to handle it.

My cock aches in my boxers, rubbing against the soft fabric, taking pleasure in the small amount of friction as I roll around in bed. I groan out loud, completely frustrated. I don't know if there can be anything between Callie and me, but my body wants it more than anything.

I can't stop thinking of the way her eyes sparked when I mentioned how often I think about her, naked in bed underneath me. She looked like she wanted me too. She looked like she wants me, just as I want her, but I try to convince myself that I saw wrong, because that's easier than thinking we could actually be something.

I think about her, in the other room, so fucking close to me, under the covers in nothing but skimpy pajamas, probably without a bra, her tits looking phenomenal –Jesus Christ– I wish I hadn't let that thought cross my mind. My hand moves to stroke my cock without even thinking about it, knowing how badly I need it, how badly I need to get her out of my system.

"Ah, fuck," I whisper, my hand stroking slowly, just giving myself a little bit of pressure. I pretend it is Callie's hand, teasing me, seeing if I would beg for her touch, and honestly, I absolutely would.

I stroke harder, running my hand down the length of my cock, the soft skin against the rough skin on my hand, making me suck in a breath as pleasure works down my spine, my vision going blurry. I feel precum leak out, not even fucking caring if I make a mess. The only thing I can think about is Callie, her body consuming my every fucking waking thought.

This is the only time I let her consume me without pushing it away. With my hand on my cock, this is the only time I give into how I'm feeling, admitting that I want her laid out in front of me, legs spread, pussy glistening with wetness.

I stroke faster, feeling myself getting close, knowing I won't last long once I start thinking of Callie naked in my bed. I imagine sliding my cock in between her pussy lips, just allowing myself to feel how fucking wet she is. I imagine her back arching, her tits bouncing with the movement. I imagine her face, as she finally, fucking finally, takes my cock inside of her. I imagine her pussy squeezing around it, her eyes rolling to the back of her head as I fuck her senselessly, just needing to feel her around me, desperation taking over any sanity that I had before she walked into my life.

I pump my cock harder, knowing I'm right on the edge but wanting to draw it out, wanting to continue thinking about Callie, continue with the fantasy.

There's a knock at my door, but I barely hear it, completely consumed with my cock in my hand, desperately pumping while thinking about my best friend, spread out in front of me.

"Hey, I couldn't sleep," Callie says with a soft voice, her head poking into the room, her mouth instantly forming an "O" as she takes in the scene in front of her.

The second I heard her voice I rush to remove my hand, but I know it's too late. I know she saw everything that I was doing. I sit up, trying to hide my rock-hard cock under the blanket, but now it is just tenting vertically, blood rushing to my face from complete and utter embarrassment.

"I wasn't doing anything," I blurt out. Genius. As if that is going to fix the situation. You fucking idiot. As if she is going to unsee everything she just saw, by pretending I wasn't doing anything. I huff out a breath, realizing that I've been doing a lot of pretending lately.

She stares at me for a second, her mouth still open, shock taking over her body. I just watch her, wide-eyed, not knowing what to do other than sit here like an dumbass.

"Fuck it," Callie finally mutters as she fully enters the room. She turns her back on me to close the door, closing it slowly as if she is convincing herself. She pushes the door until it clicks into place, then she turns the lock. That click is the only sound radiating through the room, like a bell. I stare at her as she turns around, facing me again.

The room is eerily quiet. It's quiet enough that I can feel my erratic heartbeat drumming inside me. My cock continues to pulse under the covers to the same beat, only harder since she entered the room.

Callie starts moving closer to me, her body moving across the room. I look at her confused: unable to think when I was so close to cumming to the thought of her, and now she's here. The only thought in my brain is how badly I want her, how badly I want to just give in, finally, and have her lips on mine and her body to myself.

"What are you doing?" I ask as she gets closer, needing some kind of answer about what is about to happen. I expect her to want to talk about this and what she just saw. I expect her to ask me what is happening between us and why we can't seem to stop the enviable, but instead of saying anything, instead of asking me what is going on with us or asking what I want from her, she places her hands on my chest and pushes me down, until I am laying on my back again. I stare up at her with wide eyes. She lifts the blanket, her brown hair falling between us as she climbs between the covers and on top of me, straddling me.

I feel myself gulp, still barely processing what is happening. We have been on the edge of this for so long; it feels fragile, like I could break it with only my words.

My cock rubs against the core of her body, her heat the only thing I can feel. Her eyes widen as she grinds on me, her hips moving just barely, feeling how rock-hard I am, just for her. I stare at her brown eyes, completely transfixed, completely enveloped in her, desperate for more and more and more and more.

I can feel something snapping inside of me: something that has been holding me back from doing this– from finally letting Callie in and letting the insecurity and jealousy go. I can feel how badly I want her, and I don't want to keep it a secret anymore. I can't pretend that I don't want her body, her mind, and her whole fucking soul to completely claim me. I can't pretend I don't want to taste the soft skin on her tits while she bounces up and down on my cock. I can't pretend that I'm not counting the seconds until I can be inside of her, feeling her tighten around me as she finds her pleasure in my cock, using me like a fucking toy for her desires.

"What are you doing?" I ask again, my voice hoarse with need. I stare at her body, unable to take my eyes away. She changed into the pajamas some time within the last few hours, and I know already that she isn't wearing a bra. Her plump tits sit in front of me, making my mouth literally water as I imagine them in my mouth. Her nipples are hard, and I know that if I just reached up a few feet, I could feel her tits in my hands, the weight of them, the soft skin, her hard nipples between my fingers. My cock throbs at the thought and I will myself to calm down, knowing I'm still on the edge of cumming from jerking off and having Callie on top of me, her warm pussy pressed against me, makes it that much harder to keep from chasing that release.

Callie leans down, placing her hands beside my head, bracing her weight as she looms over me. The fabric of her shirt touches my bare chest, the weight of her tits rests against me, and a groan escapes my mouth as my cock throbs, precum leaking out of the tip. "Have you ever fucked a woman, Jace?" she asks, her voice a soft whisper next to my ear, her breath hits the sensitive skin on my neck, and my balls tighten. My hands grasp the sheets next to me, as I hang on for dear life. I have imagined this scenario so many times in my fantasies, and the only reason I know that I'm awake is even when I would jerk my cock off to this exact thought, it never felt as good as this.

She leans back a little, just enough that I can look into her eyes and see that she is waiting for my answer. My heart beats fast in my chest, anticipation running through me. The idea of finally opening up, telling the secret that I haven't told anyone, feels weird, feels foreign, but I know she needs the truth, once and for all.

She leans in again, her plump lips coming close to my ear as she holds herself above me. Her tits press into my chest again, and I groan, realizing how amazing it feels to have her pressed against me. My hips lift, my cock grinding against her without thought, desperate to get any friction she is willing to give. "Have you ever felt someone's cunt lower onto your cock, taking the whole thing? Bouncing up and down, and milking you until you cum inside of them?" she whispers, and I lose my fucking mind. I don't have time to think before strings of cum cover the front of my boxers. Cum leaks out of my cock before I can stop it. Groans leak from my mouth as I release, my hands gripping the sheets as white-hot pleasure works through my body. The smell of Callie all around me only heightens my pleasure. Callie owns me as I cum for her, groaning her name over and over again, unable to stop myself.

I feel myself grind against her, desperate to prolong the pleasure. Even through her pajama shorts, I can feel her heat. She gasps as I grind against her, the entire situation feeling surreal.

I start to come down, panting and already desperate for more. My eyes find Callie's instantly, needing to know this is real. A wave of euphoria passes through me, but reality starts to sink in about what just happened. Shame starts to work through my body, knowing I just came in my fucking boxers before I even got a chance to fucking touch her. I try to push the shame away, not wanting to deal with it, but it doesn't work until I look at Callie.

She isn't looking at me with disappointment. She is looking at me with such lust and desperation that I almost think she wants me to do it again. Her eyes hold a fire I haven't seen before, and it lights my body up, making me want to do anything to please her, to pull that fire from inside of her.

She shocks me even more when she rises from straddling me, sitting on the edge of the bed next to me. The cold air hits my skin instantly, and she drags the blanket off of me, forcing a shiver down my spine. Dread runs through my blood instantly. I try to sit up, wanting to apologize for fucking this up, wanting to apologize for making such a fool out of myself, but she pushes me down again, just like she did when she first entered the room. My back hits the mattress again, and my eyes plead with her, desperate to make things better.

Her eyes run down my body, the wetness of my boxers too obvious in the moonlight dancing through the window. A fresh wave of shame washes through me, making it hard to look at her. She places her hands on my chest, the warmth of her skin instantly contrasting the chill in the air.

"God, you made such a fucking mess, didn't you?" she asks, her lips forming a pout. When she talks, my cock stirs. I nod quickly, desperate to please her, desperate to make her happy, desperate to give her the right answer. "I should probably clean it up for you, shouldn't I?" she asks, her face looking innocent while the meaning of her words sink in. I choke out a reply, barely able to speak, barely able to think, as my cock throbs, desperate to feel her mouth wrapped around my cock, sucking the cum off of it.

She moves her hands down my body, scrapping her nails against the hard plains of my stomach, leaving a sting in their place, only making me harder. I've never been one to be able to get hard after an orgasm, but it doesn't seem to matter when

Callie is involved. It feels like I could go all night. She reaches the band of my boxers, slipping her hands under slowly, so slowly that I have to resist the urge to beg, to plead for her to put me out of my misery, to finally give me the thing I have been desperate for. She slides my boxers down, taking her time, and I groan, unable to stop myself. I feel my hard cock rub against the fabric, wet with my cum, something that probably shouldn't be erotic but is. My cock springs free, wetness coating it tip to base, and I feel my cheeks redden but don't have enough of my brain to process it, too consumed by the look on Callie's face as she stares at my cum soaked cock like she wants this more than I do.

Callie leans closer to me again, her face coming close to my ear again, making me groan in frustration again, knowing she will put this off as long as possible just to drive me insane. "You want me to lick your cock clean?" Callie asks, her voice coming out like honey, sweet and innocent. Her hair grazes against my shoulder and the side of my face, goosebumps trailing down my spine. I fist the sheets, not knowing where to put my hands but wanting to touch her more than anything. I nod quickly, wanting to feel her hands on me, wanting to feel her tongue on me, on my aching cock, but not knowing if I would even be able to form the words even if I tried.

"Say please," she says, her voice holding a challenge and confidence that I have never heard before. She rises just enough that we can make eye contact, and she challenges me with her eyes, knowing how badly I want this, how badly I need this. I stare into her brown eyes, seeing a completely different person from the best friend I've had for years, and I push the small amount of fear inside of me away, knowing that it's just Callie. She knows me better than I know myself. I might not know what I'm doing, but if there is anyone I want to be doing this with, it's her.

"Please," I mutter, my voice sounding weak and hoarse. "Please suck my cock," I say, clearing my throat, knowing that I probably sound pathetic, but even the idea of that, of sounding pathetic, of sounding desperate for her, just turns me on more. I just want her touch, her mouth, her cunt. I just want to finally admit how badly I want her and how much I have thought about this moment with her. I want to stop pretending that I don't want her, because I have never wanted anyone like I want her, and she deserves to know it.

"Good boy," she says with a small smile, my eyes drawn to her lips instantly. I soak in the approval, loving the feeling of knowing I did a good job, specifically knowing I did a good job for her. Callie leans forward, settling her weight on the bed next to me and bracing her arm on my thigh, leaning forward just enough to put her head a few inches above my cock, and it jumps in anticipation. I will myself to calm down, not wanting to cum again before she has even touched it, but seeing her with her lips mere inches away, licking her lips in anticipation, makes it hard to stop myself from cumming on the spot.

She moves slowly, rubbing her hands over the parts of my thighs that aren't sticky, making my skin prickle. She lowers her head, low enough that I can feel her breath on the tip, and I bite my lip, holding back a moan as pleasure already rips through me. I don't care about anything else other than her. I only focus on her, desperate to stay present and soak in this moment.

She sticks her tongue out, moving closer, and a strangled breath comes out of me, jerking my hips upwards, my body practically begging her to *finally* put me out of my misery. Her tongue touches the head of my cock, and my head falls back against my pillow as pleasure works up my spine. Her tongue is warm and wet and everything I imagined. She swipes her tongue right under the tip, on the sensitive skin. My balls tighten as she slides back and forth, teasing me.

She sucks the head into her mouth, hollowing her cheeks, and I groan, not being able to hold back, not wanting to stop, needing her to know how much I am enjoying this, how good she makes me feel. I've never imagined that I'd be this vocal. I've enjoyed jacking off, sure, but it is nothing compared to the woman I have been thinking about for months, with her mouth on the tip of my cock, licking the cum off.

"Hold my hair, baby," she says, her voice gentle and commanding, and I soak in the term of endearment, enjoying the way it easily glides off of her tongue more than I would admit. I release my hands from the sheets, grabbing her hair out of her face, fisting it in my hand right above her head, becoming a makeshift ponytail while she bobs on my cock, sucking cum into her mouth and stroking my cock with her mouth all at once.

"Holy fuck, that is so good," I mutter, not even knowing how to explain how amazing this feels, how close I am to cumming again. I make eye contact with her as she runs her tongue down my shaft, licking the cum off of my balls. The urge to cum hits me suddenly, and I barely stop it, squeezing my eyes shut at the last possible second. Profanity leaks out of my mouth, letting her know how fucking close I was, and how badly I want to show her what she is doing to me.

She keeps sucking, and I keep getting two seconds away from another orgasm, but every time I'm on the edge, she backs off, removing her mouth from me and licking around my cock and on my thighs, cleaning the cum off other parts of me so that I can come back down to earth. She keeps pulling me back from the edge, right when I'm about to fall. Fuck. She knows exactly what she is doing.

I groan as she starts sucking the tip again, something she's found that drives me completely wild. She rubs her tongue in circles, going around the tip of my cock, making me see stars so bright that I can't concentrate on anything. She pulls back again, and I groan, loudly, aware of only Callie and her mouth. She looks at me with a smirk and the devil in her eyes as I try to catch my breath. "You need to be quiet. Someone could hear you," she mutters, her evil little mouth coaxing my cock like I could have never even imagined, getting me so close to blowing my cum in her mouth that I have no control over my own mouth anymore. I can't stop the noises, even if I fucking wanted to, even if I cared if anyone heard us.

"Callie," I say her name with desperation on my tongue, my hips jerking uncontrollably, forcing my cock an extra inch into her mouth, an extra inch that makes my vision go blurry. "Your mouth feels like fucking heaven. I don't give a fuck who hears us," I mutter, as she takes my cock deep, holding eye contact with me while the tip hits the back of her throat, and I feel myself teeter over the edge, seconds away from cumming but, again, she pulls back, the cold air pushing my orgasm away instantly, and I groan. "Please let me cum," I beg, my voice weak and hoarse. "Please," I mutter, looking up at her with complete and utter surrender, knowing I am completely at her mercy right now. She rubs her fingers under the tip of my cock, right in the spot that drives me fucking wild, while she looks at me with innocent eyes that make me want to cum on her pretty little face.

"Oh, you want to cum?" she asks, coy as fuck. Acting as if she has never even thought of the idea. She starts pumping my cock with her hand, jerking me off, and my head rolls back with pure bliss.

"Yes, yes, yes," I mumble, unable to even coherently form words at this point. "Fuck, yes, please," I beg as my balls tighten, her hand slowing, keeping me right on the edge–right where she wants me.

"You want to cum in my mouth?" she asks as she lifts her hand from my cock, and I hold back a literal whimper, ready to beg her to continue. My hips thrust all by themselves, small movements of complete and utter desperation: desperate to feel more of her mouth, her hand, hell any of her at this point.

I nod quickly, my body completely taking over, my mind not even working anymore. It feels like mush after being on the edge for so long.

"Then you need to shut the fuck up," she smiles, her lips parting slowly as her mouth drops back down to my cock. Her cheeks hollowing out as she takes my entire cock down her throat again. A loud gruntled moan leaks out of my mouth, unable to focus on her earlier commands. Her mouth releases my cock again, and she looks at me with such disapproval that I would feel bad if I had any brain cells left.

The feeling of bliss instantly leaves my body when she rises to her feet, and I worry that she is going to leave me right on the edge. Instead, she pulls her sleep shorts down quickly. I take in her body; my eyes scour every inch of her bare skin that I've never seen. She walks closer to me again with her shorts in her hand, confusing me. She stuffs them in my mouth before I have a second to say anything, and the smell of her, the taste of her, completely invades all of my senses, sending me over the edge.

She barely even gets her mouth on my cock before it starts shooting cum for the second time tonight. I release my load into her mouth, the sleep shorts quieting my moans just enough that I know Callie will be pleased, and I let go, letting the shorts swallow my groans as they come. I get lost in the pleasure, completely losing control as Callie sucks the cum out of my balls, making my entire body feel as if it is melting as white-hot pleasure shoots through it, my second orgasm more intense than the first.

I come down from my orgasm after god knows how long, my breathing coming out ragged as my vision starts to focus again. My eyes catch on Callie, needing to see her, really see her, just to ground myself back down to earth.

"Come here," I mutter, just wanting her lips on mine, finally kissing her the way I should have years ago. I want to taste her in more ways than one, but for now, I just need to feel her against me so I know this is real. I need her to put me back together after she shattered me entirely with that orgasm.

Chapter Eight

Callie

He kisses me with passion, all of his feelings releasing in that kiss, and I try to remember that this is happening, like really happening. Honestly, I think it feels like a dream just as much for him as it does for me.

I feel like something snapped inside of me, and now I'm a whole new person. I caught him jerking off his cock, and I couldn't handle the uncertainty and guessing anymore. I couldn't handle holding myself back for another second. My body yearned for him, desperation leaking from my pores, so I said fuck it. I've wanted him for so long, and I just wanted to take what I want –who I want– once and for all. I was a little nervous that he wouldn't want me, but in the back of my head, I knew the truth about what was happening between us. Learning that Jace has never fucked anyone just solidified it.

I have been waiting for him to make a move, to show me that he wants me, but I don't know if he ever would have. I think he was too scared, too unsure of himself. I have been waiting for him to confess to wanting to fuck me, but I don't even think he knows how to admit that. I'm not sure he knows how to move things from the friend zone into something more.

If I'm being honest with myself, I love knowing that I'm the first person that he has experienced this with. A primal part of me, deep inside, loves knowing that he has only ever been with me, that he is always going to remember this experience as his first time. I love knowing that I'm probably ruining him for anyone else by teasing him until he was fucking begging for me to finally let him cum.

I break the kiss, staring down at Jace, just for a second, soaking in the moment. I know he has already came twice, but I don't feel done with him. I want more from him. I have so much planned for us tonight, and I don't want it to stop now. I don't know if I want it to stop at all.

"Have you ever eaten someone out, Jace?" I ask, bringing my mouth closer to his again, our lips grazing, just barely. I feel his body shake beneath me, and it sends a thrill up my spine. My pussy starts to throb with how desperately I want him, how desperately I want to ride his face, my heat and taste soaking his tongue.

He shakes his head, looking at me with wide eyes like I just opened up his entire world, and maybe I did. I let the pride float right up to my head, allowing it to inflate my ego enough to make me feel powerful, to make me feel in control.

"Use your words," I insist, loving the way he listens to me, loving the way he holds onto every word I say as if they hold some secret he has been looking for. His eyes track my movement as I rise, my body no longer leaning over him. "Have you ever eaten someone out?" I repeat.

"No," he whispers, his voice coming out hoarse and shaky as he answers.

"Do you want to?" I ask, wanting to draw this out, wanting to make the anticipation drive him fucking insane.

"I have literally never wanted anything more than in my entire life than to taste your cunt on my tongue," he mutters, his eyes holding promise and certainty, and those feelings rush straight to my core. "Let me taste you," he whispers desperately. "Please," he begs, and I feel my pussy throb, desperate to give in and give him what he wants, what we both want.

"Move your body down," I say, my voice commanding, strong, powerful. He moves down a few inches, and I wave for him to move more, knowing I'm going to need more room for my legs if I sit on his face. Wetness pools between my legs even thinking about it, thinking about his tongue finding my clit and letting me grind against him, using him for my own pleasure.

He adjusts himself down far enough that I'm confident I will have room to do what I have planned, and I waste no time, needing to feel his tongue against my pussy more than I need to breathe.

I swing one of my legs across his chest, settling both my knees against his shoulders, placing my pussy directly above his mouth, giving him perfect access. His tongue juts out instantly, roughly sliding across my clit. His tongue is too stiff, and he moves it aimlessly, with no real rhyme or reason.

"Softer," I coax, leaning forward and trying to angle myself for him, trying to show him what I want, what I need. He brings his hands up and wraps them around my ass, squeezing and kneading, pulling me closer and bringing me deeper to his mouth. I moan at the contact and his willingness to eat me out. In front of me, I see his cock get hard for the third time. I resist the urge to suck it, not knowing if he will be able to get hard after another orgasm.

His tongue keeps swiping back and forth, his movements unsure. I can feel the anxiety in his body, the need to please me but the uncertainty, his lack of experience showing.

"Just stick your tongue out, baby. I'm gonna show you how I like it,' I say, knowing he needs this, knowing he needs me to show him what I want, and knowing that he gets off on it.

He holds his tongue against my clit, not too stiff and not too soft, and I grind my body back and forth, using his tongue to push myself closer to an orgasm. I grab his hands from my ass, bringing them up to my tits, sliding them under my tank top, letting him feel me completely. I feel his groan from under me, the sound causing a vibration against my clit that has me seeing stars already.

I look forward, watching his cock literally throb, a small pool of pre-cum gathering across his lower abdomen, right below his belly button, and the sight only heightens my pleasure. Knowing that he is getting off on this, knowing that he is leaking cum because he is so turned on while eating me out, makes my toes start to curl.

Jace squeezes my nipples between his fingers under my shirt, and I groan, feeling my orgasm start to build inside of me.

He keeps my nipples between his fingers, adding pressure that makes my back arch. I keep riding his face, my orgasm inching closer and closer as I use his tongue, treating him like my own fuck toy.

"Fu-uck, that's so good," I gasp, my body moving without thought now, my orgasm so close, close enough that I can almost feel it. I feel Jace mutter a reply, but it is muffled by my pussy, but still, it sends more vibrations to my clit, making my entire body start to shake, pleasure making me completely lose control.

My back bends forward as I lose the ability to hold myself up as I get seconds away from cumming, rubbing my clit across his tongue, showing him exactly what I like. I feel his hands on my back before I even notice they left my tits, his warm fingers wrapping around my waist and holding me up. It is somehow romantic and erotic at the same time, and I feel myself fall over the edge, unable to hold back any longer.

Pleasure wraps its way around my entire body, dulling every single one of my senses. I don't even feel like a real person for a moment, just a vessel for the pleasure ripping through it. The only thing I can think, process, and feel is the pleasure as my pussy pulses on Jace's face, unable to hold back the sounds coming from my mouth.

I feel his tongue lapping me up, sucking and licking my pussy like his life depends on it. As if this moment is as good for him as it is for me. He seems to absorb pleasure from my body just like I do from him. I gain control of my legs and muscles, my vision coming back fuzzy at first, and I take in the scene in front of me.

Jace is still holding me up, his hands wrapped around my torso. My nails are dug into his arms as I use them to hold myself steady. My breathing comes out ragged as I try to catch my breath. He keeps licking, softer now, wringing all of the pleasure out of me.

I take a deep breath, and climb off, the cold air hitting my skin and making a chill run over my body. I stand up, my legs feeling wobbly as I try to catch my balance. I turn, facing Jace as he sits up in bed, resting his weight on his forearm, a dopey smile on his face as I brace myself for the comment that I know he is about to make.

"Can you stand?" he said, his voice dripping with self-satisfaction. His voice is cocky, playful. It reminds me of the person I have been friends with for so long, the person that I don't want to lose if this situation goes south. For the first time since I walked into this room, a small wave of doubt washes over me.

"What just happened?" Jace asks, his eyes looking at me with concern. I stare at him, in only a pajama top, my nipples still hard, my pussy practically dripping, and I feel exposed, like I just played all of my cards. He wipes his face, wiping away any remnants that I was there at all.

"I don't want to ruin our friendship," I mumble, not knowing what to do. I want Jace. I want him to feel what it is like to be inside of someone, what it feels like to fuck someone until both of you shatter completely, but I don't want things between us to change. I don't want to lose him in the process of this.

"It won't ruin anything," he says, his voice uncertain. We watch each other, the room filled with tension, both of us unsure of our next move, but the longer we sit there, the more I just want to let myself sink into him, finally giving all of myself.

At this point, we have come this far, and I don't want to wake up tomorrow with any regrets left in this room. I want to give him everything, every piece of me. I want to try to make this work, even if it is doomed from the start. I want to let myself fall, completely free fall while we figure out what this means for us.

I rush forward, our lips crashing together as we consume each other, as we leave caution to the wind and just allow ourselves to be reckless, to finally have the freedom we have wanted for years.

I lean over him again, swinging my legs over his body so I can straddle him. His cock rests against my pussy, rock-hard and ready for me. Both of our bottom halves are bare, so it rests against my cunt, but I don't put it in. Instead, I just start sliding it against my pussy, getting it wet. I take a second to be thankful that I'm on the pill, not wanting anything between us. The pool of pre-cum against his lower abdomen floods my clit with moisture, making it slick as I grind on his pelvis. I'm still sensitive since my last orgasm, and already, I feel another building inside of me.

I sit up straight, breaking our kiss, and take my top off, finally exposing my entire body to the cold air and to Jace's gaze. He drinks my body in, his eyes seeming to get lost in me. He looks up and down, his eyes trailing me entirely, and then does it again, getting caught on my tits, on my hard nipples a few times, unable to take his gaze away.

"Do you want to fuck me, Jace?" I ask, my voice like honey, sweet and tempting. I lean over him, my hands resting on the bed right above his shoulders, and my tits resting only mere inches from his face.

The tip of his cock connects with my entrance, and I know that if I just moved my body down, he would be inside of me, but I wait, knowing I want him to be on the edge before he is allowed to fuck me, to feel my tight cunt wrapping around him.

"Y-yes," he groans, his voice shaky, the desire in his voice obvious. He grasps the sheets again, probably not knowing where to put his hands, and one by one, I move them to my ass, letting him get a good feel. He groans, his head tipping back as he mutters curse words that I can barely hear.

"That didn't sound very convincing. Maybe you don't want it after all," I say, my lips forming a pout as I look into his eyes. His eyes panic at the prospect of me leaving him like this. I move my leg, as if I am going to get up and resist him, but his hands hold me steady.

"No, please," he begs, his voice completely desperate, looking at me as if I hung the fucking moon. "I want this so fucking bad," he pleads, his fingers digging into my ass as I settle myself back in his lap, his cock still against my cunt, my wetness slowly dripping down his cock.

"You want what?" I tease, needing to hear him say it. "Tell me what you want me to do to you." I lean close, my tits against his chest, my lips against his ear, and my cunt against his cock.

Our bodies are perfectly lined up, ready for him to take, but he waits, waits for me to tell him what to do.

"Jesus Christ," he mutters, his voice low, desire radiating through his entire body. His hips thrust, just barely, not enough to start fucking me, but just enough to make my pussy ache with desperation, lusting to have him inside of me. "I want you to fuck me," he says, his eyes hopeful, hopeful that I will finally give in, give him what he wants. Instead, I tilt my head to the side, looking at him with my eyebrows raised.

"That's not good enough," I respond, moving to get off again, but this time he is ready for me and his hands pin me in place right on top of him.

"I want you to use this cock, use it to make yourself cum, and then fuck me until I cum inside of you. I want you dripping with my cum. I want to see it running down your leg after you're done with me," he says, his voice so fucking eager, so fucking rushed. I pretend to think about it, like I ever stood a chance of walking away. I wouldn't have the ability to stop right now, not when we are so close to getting what we both want.

"Good boy," I whisper in his ear, feeling him smile at my words before I sink his cock inside of me, taking it deep, as deep as I can.

Chapter Nine

Jace

Jesus fucking Christ, I'm going to cum. I'm going to cum instantly. Holy fucking shit, she is so fucking warm and tight, and I'm going to fucking cum if she doesn't stop right now.

She lowers herself until she is balls deep, my entire cock inside of her, pulsing with desire, my balls tightening, ready to cum at any second. She lifts her entire body until she is sitting up again, her tits right at my eye level, and my mouth waters. What I wouldn't give to have her tits in my mouth, her hard nipples against my tongue while she rides my cock just how she likes it.

I will myself to stop thinking about it, knowing it is going to send me over the edge, knowing it is going to make me cum too fast. I want to hold out for her. I want to be good for her. I just want her approval like I've never wanted anything else.

The thought hits me suddenly– I'm having sex right now. I'm no longer a virgin. It feels almost surreal. I better not be fucking dreaming. I hope to god I'm not. I've had this dream a few times before, and I hope this time it is real, because, Jesus Christ, she feels like fucking heaven with her cunt wrapped around me.

"You feel so good inside of me," she gasps, moving her hips up and down, using me to build her pleasure. I resist the urge to let my eyes roll back, not wanting to miss a second of the sight above me. Her tits bounce as she moves, and I dig my fingers into her ass, knowing she may have marks in the morning but not fucking caring. I want her to have a reminder of what happened between us. I know I'm going to remember this for the rest of my fucking life. Her hair sweeps in front of her face, but she doesn't stop. She doesn't stop fucking me. She just keeps fucking bouncing, moving her hair out of the way, until its behind her back.

She tips her head back, the sight of her entire body on display, and I –for the billionth time tonight– hold back the urge to cum, seeing her tits and stomach and face without anything covering her. I knew sex would feel good but watching a goddess on top of me, churning her own pleasure out of my body, feels like an out-of-body experience.

"I'm going to cum if you keep going," I moan, more of a warning than anything else. I don't want to disappoint her. I don't want to finish before she says so, but I don't know if I can stop myself. I want to make her cum first. I want her to enjoy this, but it feels so fucking good I don't even think I'm going to be able to stop myself if she keeps going.

"Jace, I am so close already, just don't fucking cum," she urges, her voice desperate for the first time tonight, and it lights something inside of me. I lift my hips, fucking her too, our hips connecting together at the same time, making a slapping sound with our skin that vibrates through the entire room. I thrust my hips without thought, needing more of her, needing all of her, needing her to feel what I feel.

"Holy shit," she groans, her pussy tightening as she continues to bounce on my dick. "Rub my clit," she says, looking into my eyes when she tells me what to do. I move one of my hands from her ass to her clit, not knowing exactly what to do but knowing I need to figure it out because I can't hold on much longer. I try to replicate the movements she enjoyed when my tongue was on her cunt, but I can't seem to get it right. I look up at her, worry in my eyes as I rub aimlessly, not knowing what the fuck I'm doing.

She moves to hold herself up with one hand, grinding on my cock, moaning louder, her body moving quickly and with purpose. She places her free hand on top of mine and moves my fingers the way she likes, the way she needs. I follow her every direction, paying attention to which motions make her moan, and which motions make her pussy clench against me. She keeps her hand directly above mine, guiding me as we fuck each other, a sweaty bundle of limbs both at the edge of orgasm.

My orgasm blooms inside of me, but I hold it back, trying my best to take my mind off of it, knowing I need to hold out for her. A deep moan comes out of her, her fingers picking up the pace against her clit, and her legs seem to give out. She stops moving, seemingly overtaken by pleasure, but I keep fucking her, needing to feel more, needing to feel all of her, needing to experience this with her.

"Oh my god, I'm going to cum," she whispers, her voice hoarse, her voice needy. Her legs start shaking, and her pussy tightens, her orgasm taking her entire body by storm, but I keep going, staring at her, taking it all in, loving every. fucking. second.

Her head tips back, her eyes roll back in ecstasy, and her legs shake in front of me as she gets lost in the pleasure. Her nipples pebble, and I lick my lips, desperate for a taste. Our sweaty skin slaps together, and the sound echoes through the room, and in this moment, I almost hope someone hears it. I want everyone to know that she is mine. I want everyone to know that I claimed her just as much as she claimed me. After this, she is the only person I'm going to be able to think about when my cock gets hard.

And that's the thought that sends me over the edge, straight into my third orgasm for the night. I feel my cum coat the inside of her pussy as pleasure takes me by storm. I mumble words that probably have no meaning as Callie leans down, her chest connected with mine, and she takes my lips in hers, running her tongue against my lips until I open up for her.

We kiss while I cum inside of her, completely overtaken with pleasure and emotion, something I have never experienced before. She holds my head with her hands while her tongue speaks to me with actions instead of words.

Chapter Ten

Callie

I roll off of him, completely exhausted. The entire night has been exhausting, but this has worn me out completely, taking every ounce of energy from my body and wringing it out. I want to talk about so much with him, to finally understand what the fuck is happening between us, but now my emotions feel completely fried.

"Jesus Christ," he mutters, a small laugh vibrating through his chest and warming the room, and I smile despite myself. He looks over at me, and our eyes connect. He looks at me with such amazement, such adoration, and I feel butterflies erupt in my stomach, not knowing what we are supposed to do now.

I took the lead, and I liked it, but I need him to want me too. I need him to express how he wants more with me, how he wants this to be more than just a one-time thing, because that's what I want.

I've had a thing for him for years, and even though it has been mostly physical, a part of me has always wondered what we would be like in a relationship, but I can't keep making the moves. At some point, he needs to want this too, and that scares me. I don't like putting the ball in his court because I am worried he is going to fuck it up, but I know that I can't initiate this conversation. I am going to have to trust him.

"Well," I sigh, lifting my body from the bed, all of my muscles sore. I look around for my clothes, thinking of going back to my guest room and sleeping for the next twenty years. I glance around the floor, finding my sleep shorts, wet from Jace's mouth, but I put them on anyway, sliding them on quickly, feeling the need to cover up.

"Wait, what is going on?" Jace asks, his voice afraid and completely confused. I turn back toward him, my tits still out, half of my body still exposed, and it feels different now, more vulnerable in the moonlight after what we just did, when I'm unsure of what he wants with me after I used his body for my own pleasure.

"I'm going back to my room," I shrug, finding my shirt on the other end of the room and grabbing it quickly, wanting to cover as much of myself as possible. Usually, sex doesn't feel this vulnerable afterward, but this feels like I just gave him everything, like I exposed every secret I have ever kept.

"You're not going to stay?" he asks, his question coming out like what we are is obvious. Like he knows exactly what we are, but none of this is obvious. I have no idea what is going on between us, and I wish that I did. I wish he would shout from the rooftops what he wants right now, so I could at least attempt to make some sense of this situation. I pull my shirt on, not even knowing how to answer him.

"You want me to stay?" I ask, unsure. I don't mean to sound insecure. I just don't know where we stand. I just want to know what is happening right now, because while he acts all nonchalant, my insides feel like they are being eaten alive.

"Of course I do," he huffs, as if I should have understood, as if he said something to me that would indicate that this is more than just a hookup to him, more than just a person to lose his virginity to. I hate to admit it but it was more for me, and now that I'm clothed and thinking clearly, I don't know what I'm going to do if he doesn't feel the same.

"I don't know if I should," I hesitate, uncertainty wrecking through me. Does he want me to stay because he wants someone to fuck in the morning, someone to keep the bed warm until the dawn breaks, and then we pretend nothing happened between us, like this night doesn't exist in both of our memories, or does he want me to stay because he wants to be with me, to see what can happen between us. I feel my mind spiraling–trying to analyze everything simultaneously.

Jace looks at me, completely bewildered, like I'm speaking a different language, and he has no idea what I'm even talking about. His face morphs from confusion to anger quickly, and he looks at me with bunched eyebrows and a scowl. "Was this just a hook-up to you?" he spits out, as if the words in his mouth disgust him, as if his words are vile.

I know the answer to his question, but it's scary to say it. I was so confident a few minutes ago, when his cock was out and I was horny, but it feels different when the post-orgasm high has worn off. It feels different when I'm standing in front of him, cold, not knowing what he wants with me after we fucked.

"Was it just a hook-up to *you*?" I ask, genuinely curious, not knowing the answer. I don't know why it is so hard for me to think about this going anywhere. I'm so nervous that he is going to fuck this up. I've wanted to be in his bed for years, and now that is happening, I'm not sure how to trust it.

"Of course not!" he exclaims, his voice loud, booming through the room and echoing off the walls. Jace rips off the covers, his face tinted red, and then stands up, finding his boxers on the floor and putting them on quickly, his movements rapid and angry. "I've wanted to do that for months, Callie. You have completely taken over my thoughts for *months,* and now you are going to give me a taste and tell me it meant nothing to you?" he asks quickly, angrily. His voice demands attention, and I listen. I watch his every movement, my eyes trained on him like they always have been, unable to tear them away.

His words click through me, and relief washes through me, the anxiety rushing away, leaving me with a feeling of happiness, of hope that we could become something outside of this room.

"I didn't say that," I say, looking him in the eyes, a small part of me knows what this means, what this will become between us, and it scares me, but I'm sick of living in fear of this. We are so close. I'm sick of being scared that this won't work out or it will ruin the friendship. I just want to do what the hell I want for once.

"You didn't say what?" Jace spits out, looking away from me as if he can't even stand to look at me anymore. I step closer to him and take a breath. I push every ounce of fear out of my body.

"I didn't say that it didn't mean anything to me," I say, looking up at him, willing him to understand my words, willing him to see what I see. His movements stop as he comprehends my words, turning back toward me, and really looking at me. He analyzes my face for the truth, realization slowly dawning on his face.

"I don't want this to be a one-time thing, Callie. I want to figure out what the hell this could be between us," he says, his hands connecting with my waist as he steps closer to me, his fingers grabbing onto me as if he fears that I will disappear out of thin air, but I understand the feeling.

"Me too," I say, feeling vulnerable and exposed but knowing that I need to be, knowing that it will be the only way to finally become more than just friends, something that I didn't even know that I wanted so badly until this night with him.

"I don't know what is going to happen between us, but can we just agree that we are going to try to figure it out?" Jace asks, his eyes holding fear and uncertainty as he stares at me, waiting for an answer.

"Yeah, we can do that," I reply, bringing my head down on his chest, just holding him for a second as his arms wrap around me. Both of us breathe and just soak in the moment. Then I climb back into his bed, needing a couple hundred hours of sleep to recover from the highs and lows of emotions I went through today. Jace's arm drapes over me, and I back my ass up until it rests against his cock, and I feel it harden instantly. "Seriously? Again?" I say, laughing, my voice tired. I feel my body shift, so his mouth is right above my ear, his breath against my skin.

"I don't think you realized that the second you locked the door, you became mine, Callie. You claimed me just as much as I claimed you," he whispers, his cock grinding against me and his hand coming around my body, his fingers instantly finding my nipple while all of the exhaustion seeps out of my body and desire replaces it.

It's going to be a long night if we keep going like this, but something tells me this won't be the last long night we have, at least if I have anything to say about it.

Epilogue

Callie

I sit by the pool in a reclining chair, the sun basking on my skin, heating me from the inside out. I glance over at Jace, his shirt over his eyes in a makeshift eye mask, as he tans under the sun with me. I try not to stare, I really do, but my eyes cling to him, my amazement for him not wavering even after all this time.

I remember the days when I wished our friendship would become more, when I was so desperate for something else from him, to finally cross that line that we were both so fucking scared to cross, and here we are, on the other side, and I've never been happier.

My eyes skate over his body, just memorizing it, just soaking in it, appreciation radiating through my whole being. Sometimes I feel so fucking lucky, so lucky that we found our way to each other, that we worked through all the bullshit holding us back, that we finally got to the place we both wanted to be.

"You need to stop looking at me like that," Jace mutters and my eyes dart to his. He has lifted his shirt just enough that we can see each other, our eyes connecting in a lust-filled gaze. I smile at him, my body already responding to him, my body tuned into him so perfectly that just the tone of his voice can make me react.

"Or what?" I ask, with a raise of my eyebrow, teasing him. He groans into his shirt, and I just smile at him, loving the way I can influence him, loving the way his body constantly responds to me over the smallest fucking things. Our bodies still react like it's the first night again and we are just exploring each other for the first time, like everything is new and undiscovered still.

He takes the shirt off his eyes, mischief in his gaze as he sits up, his gaze sweeping around the pool, and I look too, trying to figure out what he is watching for. It's beautiful here, the resort has a gorgeous pool, surrounded by palm trees and plants, giving it a natural feeling, and it opens directly into the lobby, giving it an indoor-outdoor atmosphere, making you feel luxurious while still giving you just enough privacy.

Of course, we didn't pay for this. Finn and Emma's wedding was a few days ago, and they flew everyone out here and paid for a week of rooms for everyone, wanting to have a little vacation before they went and traveled for a few months. It's insanely generous, but I'm forbidden from thanking them again, their orders. I guess ten times is a few too many. Who would have thought? It's not like they can't afford it, but it feels so weird to be thrust into this life, with the perfect man, on the perfect vacation. Sometimes it feels too good to be true, like I'm dreaming, and I'm going to open my eyes and be back in the friend zone with Jace, wishing we could be more.

I watch as Jace continues to look around, and I quirk my eyebrow at him, trying to figure out what he's looking at, but before I can ask, he's climbing out of his chair, walking the step or two over to me, climbing on top of my recliner so his body is over mine, and taking my chin in one hand, while he holds himself up with the other, and connecting his lips to mine.

I kiss back, swept away by the feel of him, his body pressing against me in the chair, his pelvis pressed against mine, his erection pressing against my leg as his tongue sweeps into my mouth. I pull away, remembering where we are, my cheeks reddening at the thought of someone seeing us, catching us in this position.

"Jace," I scold. "There are people here," I say in a whisper, looking around, finding no one; the pool completely empty beside us, and the lobby empty too, everyone seemingly vanishing into thin air at the perfect moment.

"No one is here," he says in a comforting tone, his lips connecting with mine again, his tongue sweeping into his mouth, the heat of his body on top of me radiating through the thin bikini covering me. I run my hands over his smooth chest, melting back into the kiss, thankful for the easy access to him, loving the feel of his muscles against my fingers.

"God, all it takes is one look, and my cock is rock hard," Jace mutters, his mouth running down my neck, lining me with kisses. I try to stay quiet, not wanting to alert anyone, but it's hard with his mouth all over me. "Please don't make me stop," he begs, his mouth close to my ear, close enough that I can feel his breath against my skin, and I shiver. "I can't fucking help myself," he mutters, his strong body on top of me, completely consuming every inch of me, taking me hostage in his embrace. "Do you know what you do to me, Callie?" he asks, his voice hoarse, so filled with need, so desperate for me.

He grabs my hand and brings it to his cock, and I gasp lightly, his erection rock hard in my hand. I rub him up and down, teasing him with small touches and he groans into my neck, his hand running up and down my side, feeling my body under him, as if he can't get enough, as if his sole purpose on this earth is to touch me, to savor me.

He kisses down to my chest, his tongue making a trail from my mouth to my collarbones, and I arch up, offering my tits to him, desperate for him to touch me, to make me feel good, even though someone could walk in at any moment. That's the thrilling part, the part that makes anticipation run through me.

I focus on it, the fact that someone could find up like this, with my hand on his hard cock, and his tongue on my skin, his body on top of mine, and they would know exactly what we are doing, exactly what we want. It wouldn't take much for someone to see us, and I don't fucking care. I almost want that, want someone to bear witness to what we have between us, to the passion radiating in the air around us.

Jace lifts his body up, his eyes not even meeting mine, but looking at my tits, as he takes the thin material in front of my nipples and moves it to the side, exposing me to him and to the cool breeze, to the warm sun. He just sits there for a second, taking the sight in front of him, his eyes darting between my tits, pure lust filling his gaze.

"God, I'm never gonna get fucking sick of this," he mutters, before he leans back down his mouth connecting with my nipple, the heat instantly making my back arch. I grasp and pump his cock in my hand lazily, focusing on the pleasure he is giving me as his tongue flicks over my nipples, leaving them wet when he switches to the other. I feel my pelvis grind against his leg sitting in between my own. I'm desperate for anything, any kind of friction, any kind of release.

"Fuck," I mutter, his tongue flicking back and forth over my nipple. He uses his free hand to cup my tit while his tongue consumes me, claiming all of my attention. He groans into my skin, his eyes almost rolling back with how much he is enjoying this, and I just watch him, mesmerized by him, loving every second of watching him enjoy me, enjoy pleasing me.

"Your tits are fucking perfect, Callie," he mutters, his voice so fucking breathy it shoots pleasure through me, just the mere sound of his voice feeling like a touch running through my entire body, coaxing pleasure from me.

I just hum back, loving the way he is praising me, loving the way he worships me, loving the way he treats me, whether I'm naked or not, like I am a goddess and he is lucky to be seen with me. I arch my back up, desperate for him to put his mouth back on me, desperate for him to finish the job he started, but his hand on the edge of my bikini bottom grabs my attention. His fingers play with the edge of the fabric, moving it over, so fucking slowly, exposing my pussy to the warm air, the sun shining on the most intimate part of my body.

"God, I bet you're already wet, aren't you?" Jace asks his voice filled with pure desire, with desperation, like he can't wait until he can feel me, really feel me. His fingers tease my skin, tease the wetness between my legs, like he can't get enough, like he is going to die if he doesn't touch me.

I try to be quiet, try not to allow him the satisfaction of knowing how much I adore his touch, how much he makes me lose myself, but when he slips a finger inside of me, and his mouth comes back down on my nipple at the same time, I lose all my resolve, and a moan escapes me, my entire body consumed with him.

I lift my hand from his cock, and hold his head with my hands, my fingers threading through his hair as his finger pumps into my slowly, making my muscles tighten and my body clench as the pleasure builds. His tongue flicks across my nipple, and when he lifts his head up, his teeth graze it, driving me fucking wild.

He switches to the other nipple, taking his finger out, and adding another, and the added pressure makes me sit right on the edge, and he fucking knows it. He can read my body now, knows how to keep me right on the edge, but keeps me from barreling over, from sinking into the pleasure. He knows he is going to pay for this later, and that just makes him want to do it more.

He fingers me slowly, so fucking slow that it feels like torture, his mouth around my nipple, barely giving me enough sensation, barely keeping me on the edge. I feel his thumb connect with my clit, and then not move, just sitting there, adding pressure, making it that much harder to keep myself from falling over the edge.

"Jesus Christ, Jace," I moan, knowing I need to be quiet, knowing I don't want anyone to hear me, but I'm so fucking close, just barely sitting on the edge, and I can't help it. I move my hips, trying my best to thrust his fingers deep inside of me, but he doesn't budge, holding my body exactly how he wants it, exactly how he needs it, so he can keep me in the palm of his hand.

"God, I fucking love you like this," he mutters, his voice filled with desire, with lust, and I know without even seeing that he's hard as a fucking rock, desperate for me to touch him, for me to finally please him the way he is pleasing me, but he knows, I'm not as nice as he is, and everything he is doing to me, I'm just gonna do to him, ten times over, make him sit on the edge for longer, make him wait for his pleasure.

His thumb rubs on my clit, just fucking barely, and I feel my orgasm starting, just the start of it, and I grab onto his hair, my head tipping back. I watch the moment his resolve breaks, when he can't take anymore waiting. This happens every time, like my orgasm is too good for him to wait, like he can't help pushing me over the edge, giving up on the idea of teasing me. "God, I can't wait any fucking longer. Please fucking cum baby. I need to see you fucking cum," he says, his resolve dissolving in front of him, his patience giving out, just like I knew it would. I feel his fingers pump into me, fast now, his impatience evident, his need to see me cum too strong, too much when I'm sitting right on the edge, and I feel my orgasm take my over, with my nipple his mouth, his fingers in my cunt, and his thumb on my clit, I cum, and I cum fucking hard, barely keeping my noises at bay, barely holding myself together enough that we don't get caught.

I come down slowly, Jace working my body just enough, his finger still pumping inside of me slowly, his thumb rubbing slow circles, enough to ride out my orgasm for as long as possible, while he watches me, watches as bliss takes over my face, watches as I fall a little deeper in love with him every fucking time.

"God, you're so fucking beautiful," he whispers, looking at me with so much adoration, so much love, that I feel myself melt into him. I didn't think I would ever get so lucky. To fall in love with someone like him, someone so amazing, so caring, and someone who gets me so fucking perfectly, who compliments me so well.

I snake my hand down his body, feeling the hard ridges beneath my palm, loving the feel of his body still against mine. I kiss him, willing him to stay put, loving the way he is blocking the sight to the lobby, meaning no one can see where my hand is traveling, giving us more privacy for all the things I have in store for us.

I reach into his swim trunks, pulling his cock out easily, just barely thrusting it in my hand, the slightest movement almost making his elbows buckle around me. I watch as his eyes start to roll back as I jerk my hand, his entire body so fucking responsive to me, so fucking worked up after watching me cum, like it is the most erotic thing he could ever witness, like my own orgasm could bring him to the edge all by itself.

"You're so fucking good at that, Callie," he mutters, his eyes looking into mine with love, with desperation, with so much emotion it makes the moment seem so much more serious than I'm ready for.

"Are you gonna be a good boy and cum all over my tits?" I ask, needing to redirect us to sex, to redirect us to his desire, because the way he is looking at me makes me want to kiss him, to make love to him, to let him fuck my body slowly until he has rung us both for all of the pleasure we have, and I'm too greedy, too antsy to make him beg for my touch, to beg for his cum.

"Fuck, don't," he whispers, his voice carrying a warning, a plea, but I just smile up at him, loving the way his body reacts to me, the way he is putty in my hand, so easy to manipulate for exactly what I need him for.

"What?" I ask with mock innocence, my mouth forming a pout and I watch as his eyes track the movement, his cock twitching in my hand as I continue to fuck it with my hand in slow strokes, giving him just barely enough to come closer to the edge, bringing him there slowly, never giving him the full satisfaction he needs.

"You know what you do to me, Callie," he mutters, his voice a whine, desperate, and I smile at him again, my own body coming alive at the sound, loving my name on his lips.

"Tell me," I demand, my voice more breathy than I wanted, but I stop caring, too needy to care right now, suddenly overtaken by hearing this. "What do I do to you?" I ask, my hand moving faster now, pushing him to tell me, rewarding good behavior, and it works because he swears under his breath, his arms starting to shake above me, but his mouth opens.

"You fucking own me, Callie," he admits, and I feel the words hit me, my entire body lighting up with desire, my love for him so fucking big it feels overwhelming, like it's too much for my body to hold anymore. "You own my body," he murmurs, "of course, you fucking do," he says with a moan, my hand still working him. "But you fucking own every piece of me. Any piece you want, it's all fucking yours," he says his brown eyes staring right back into mine, the meaning of his words so fucking clear, the emotion behind them so present between us, like it's in the air surrounding us, like it has taken the place of the oxygen and it's the only thing I can breathe now.

I keep stroking him faster, his hand moving over the ridges and veins of his cock, rounding over the tip in a way I know he fucking loves, and I watch as he sits right on the edge, right on the edge of cumming, and I watch as he tries to push it away, keep himself off the edge, but I push him closer, moving my hand faster, desperate for his release.

"Fuck, Callie I'm gonna fucking cum if you keep doing that," he says, his voice so breathy, a desperate plea for me not to stop, for me to keep going, for me to let him barrel into bliss.

"Cum," I mutter, the word barely more than a whisper. "Claim me," I say, needing him cum on my body, his mark on me, needing him to own me just as much as I own him because he does. He owns me too, he has every piece of me that he wants, and I can't take any of it back. I thought I had fallen for him before, thought I knew what it meant to love him, but I never even knew this was an option, to love him so fiercely, to love him too wholly, to love him through everything, that it doesn't matter what happens anymore. He has my heart, and I don't even want it back.

Strings of cum leak from his cock, coating my stomach in the sticky liquid, and my back arches, my tits catching all of his release while he groans lightly, keeping his noises to just the two of us, both of us still trying not to get caught, but both too keyed up to stay completely quiet. I jerk the rest of his cum out, letting the few drops fall on my hand, right between my thumb and pointer, and I bring my hand to my mouth, licking his release off while he watches, his eyes filling with desire again, already ready for more, already ready for another round, and I smile up at him, my heart so fucking full, more full than I ever imagined it could be.

"I love you," I say in a rush, needing to say the words, needing him to know how I feel. I have known the words were true for so fucking long, but I finally let them pass my lips. Jace smiles down at me, looking at me like I hung the fucking moon, like I could do no wrong, and I feel so fucking whole under his gaze.

"I love you too," he mutters, kissing me, sealing the moment before grabbing a towel to clean me up and leading me away from the pool and to our room, so we can both show each other just how much love there is between us.

Epilogue

Jace

"Hey, thanks for the trip man, it was awesome," I say, patting my brother on the back as we hug. We are standing in the lobby, a plane ticket in both of our bags, but his is for another country, and mine is back home; the vacation only starting for him and finishing for me.

"No problem, I'm glad you could make it out," he replies, pulling away from me, and I'm suddenly extremely thankful I made it out. It doesn't happen often that we get moments like this, moments where we can just hang out with each other.

"I'll see you when you get back?" I ask, already knowing it will be a few months before he's back in the country.

"Yeah, of course," he says, and I turn away, ready to go home with a new tan, but his voice catches my attention. "You do know they have cameras at the pool, right?" he asks, and when I turn to look at him, he is smirking at me, probably just happy to have something over me, something that he can use against me.

"Ah," I say, feeling my cheeks heat, embarrassed more that we got caught than anything else because I don't think there is a cell in my body that could ever regret what happened at that pool. "I didn't know that," I say, running over exactly what happened, reliving every moment, thinking about the poor soul who found that footage. I feel myself react, my cock hardening even at the thought of Callie's hand wrapped around it, milking it for everything it has.

"It's a five-star resort. They have cameras everywhere," Finn says, amusement in his tone. I shrug, my embarrassment waving, the situation seeming more funny than anything. I go to turn away again, feeling as if there is nothing more to say, but a thought strikes me, and I turn around again.

"You don't think I could get a copy of that tape, do you?"

Books By This Author

Done Right (She Teaches Him #1):

What happens when Emma, who just wants to be done right, meets Finn, who doesn't know what he's doing?

Taught Right (She Teaches Him #2):

What happens when Joey, who just wants to be taught right, hires Ava, who knows exactly how to teach him?

Greedy:

What happens when the best kind of revenge, is fucking your ex-boyfriend's business rival?

About The Author

Rhianna Burwell is an Amazon best seller in erotica. Author of the Before series and the She Teaches Him series, available on Kindle Unlimited, she takes pride in writing spicy, realistic, and deeply satisfying romance and erotica. Rhianna currently resides in Minnesota, where—when she's not writing erotica hot enough to melt all the winter snows—she enjoys curling up with her cat, avidly watching Grey's Anatomy, and reading—her current fav is alien romance. Rhianna loves to hear from readers, who can connect with via any of her social media links.

Instagram: @rhiannaburwellauthor
Tiktok: @rhiannaburwellauthor

9 781088 292983